VERITAS

Also by Mandi Jourdan:
LACRIMOSA
a novel
SHADOWS OF THE MIND
short stories

VERITAS

A Novel By

MANDI JOURDAN

Adelaide Books
New York / Lisbon
2018

VERITAS
a novel
by Mandi Jourdan

Published by Adelaide Books, New York / Lisbon
adelaidebooks.org

Editor-in-Chief
Stevan V. Nikolic

For any information, please address Adelaide Books
at info@adelaidebooks.org
or write to:
Adelaide Books
244 Fifth Ave. Suite D27
New York, NY, 10001

ISBN13: 978-1-949180-08-4
ISBN10: 1-949180-08-5

Printed in the United States of America

Chapter One

August 7, 2232

Desi eyed the slick chrome platform warily from behind the glass double-doors of the lobby where her brother had been murdered, and she did her best not to think about how close she stood to the spot where he'd taken his final breath. She had never occupied the podium in front of LDE's Manhattan office, but she'd seen far too many press conferences transmitted from it over the past few weeks for comfort.

You can do this, she told herself. *You owe it to him.*

"Are you all right, Miss Lawrence?"

Squaring her shoulders and lifting her chin, Desi looked to Captain Ryder, who stood beside another blue-suited officer just to the left of the doors. The captain's hair had gone a bit greyer since he'd been tasked with the murder case that had cost New York two of its three most famous robotics engineers and had still ended in a cold trail.

With a nod and a tight smile, Desi shifted her attention to her surviving brother Derek, who stood on the platform in front of the building addressing a crowd of reporters. The bright flashes igniting every few seconds were, Desi knew, a bad sign. If the throng was this desperate to photograph her brother now, she couldn't begin to imagine how many flashes would blind her when she joined him on the podium in time with his announcement.

You can do this.

Derek looked out of place in a suit. He'd always been the one of LDE's founders who'd taken his role the least seriously, at least in terms of dress. His heart had always been completely in his work, but he'd never wanted to be seen as a CEO. Desi recalled how often Derek had worn t-shirts while Damian, their elder brother, had been in black-tie attire, and Eddie…

Desi stopped cold, determined to keep her thoughts from progressing any further, but it was too late. She already felt the strong arm wrapped around her chest, binding her arms to her sides.

Her pulse accelerated so rapidly she had to swallow down the urge to throw up in her mouth. She took a few steps backward and clutched the nearest stable surface she could find—the security desk at the heart of the round, chrome-plated lobby.

A shiver shot through her like an electric current.

She remembered sitting at a computer after her brother's visitation service, watching the security footage of the night he'd fled for his life in this room. She'd watched as he'd vaulted over this very desk and tried the front doors only to find the building on lockdown and his exit rendered impossible.

"Miss Lawrence?"

Desi's gaze skated over the spot where Damian had lain by the front doors, bloody and broken, and to the police captain approaching her. She opened her mouth to respond, but the words died on her tongue at the sight of the captain's sidearm.

"What are you doing?" she mouthed as she felt the ghost of a gun's cold barrel pressed to her right temple.

"I'm sorry."

She heard the words in her mind as clearly as though he were speaking them now. She heard the low tenor of the voice that had comforted her when she'd lost the brother who had been more like a surrogate father to her. The voice that had eulogized him with a touching speech about one fourth-grade boy befriending another and forging a lifelong bond that had been stolen away by murder. The voice that had whispered sweet words into her ear after she'd finally let her guard down enough to admit her brother's best friend had meant more to her than a one-night stand and she'd allowed herself to fall for him again.

The voice that had whispered *"This is not what I wanted"* while the speaker had held a gun to her head.

"Miss Lawrence."

Desi hadn't registered that the warehouse had materialized before her until the stacks of shipping crates had dissolved again to give way to the lobby and the concerned, mustached face of Captain Ryder.

"Are you all right?" he asked.

"I'm fine," she muttered.

"Are you sure? Maybe you should sit down." Ryder rested a hand on her shoulder, but she shook her head.

"No, thank you. He'll be ready for me any—"

As she spoke, Derek turned on the podium and stretched out a hand toward the lobby. Through the glass, he met Desi's eyes and offered her an encouraging smile.

"Thank you," she said again to Ryder.

With a deep breath, she crossed the room to the doors and pushed them open. The quiet of the soundproof lobby was immediately drowned in a chorus of shouts for her attention and bursts of light from flashing cameras. She plastered on a smile and waved to the assembled reporters and the spectators clustered behind them.

"Today," said Derek into the microphone adjoined to the podium, "it's my pleasure to announce that I'm naming my sister Desdemona as LDE's co-president."

He took Desi's hand and gave it a reassuring squeeze, and for an instant, her smile grew more genuine. Despite the handful of robotics classes she'd taken in college, they had only been toward her minor and not her major. She held a bachelor's degree in theater, and she'd never felt that her brothers viewed her as qualified for even an entry-level position in the business they had begun with Eddie several years earlier.

She had no idea whether Derek really found her worthy or whether he simply needed someone he could trust in the position, now that one of the company's founders was dead and another was a wanted fugitive.

"I'm thrilled to have her onboard," Derek continued, "and I know she'll be an asset to our team and to our brother's legacy." He inhaled deeply. "I believe we have time to take a few questions."

Desi's stomach lurched. She'd known this was a possibility depending on how long her brother spoke, but she was still unprepared for what the reporters could ask her.

A swarm of hands shot into the air. Derek called on a woman in the first row.

"Mr. Lawrence," the reporter began, "do you feel that your sister is qualified for such a demanding position, especially given the circumstances?"

"Yes, I do," said Derek flatly. "Next?"

Desi kept her focus on the edge of the platform upon which she and Derek stood, unwilling to meet the eyes of any of the people scrutinizing her.

"Have there been any new developments in the case pertaining to Eddie Dodson?"

Desi's hands clenched involuntarily into fists, her nails biting into her palms.

"No," said Derek, "we know nothing new."

"Do you know where—?"

"No, we have no idea where he is. We have had no contact with him."

"Miss Lawrence, isn't it true that you engaged in a physical relationship with Dodson around the time of your brother's death?"

Desi's mouth went dry. She scanned the crowd at last, but with every eye fixed on her, she couldn't tell who had asked the question. The murmur of conversation had died, and beside her, Derek had frozen.

Desi knew no matter what she said, her words would be misconstrued. She couldn't admit that she'd been involved with Eddie, because then what was to stop them from accusing her of being involved in Damian's death? She couldn't deny the relationship, because she knew some photograph or video clip would emerge that incriminated her and brought further damning scandal to the company.

"No comment," said Desi. The words tasted like ash in her mouth. She turned on her heel and started back toward the lobby, ignoring the shouts and flashes that followed her.

Eddie clung to the arms of his chair so tightly his knuckles were white. He watched her go on the telesense screen, her projected image seemingly just within the range of his fingertips if he only reached out to her. She was walking away from the question about him just as she'd walked away from him when he'd fallen asleep beside her and awoken to find the space beside him empty, and the sight made his chest ache.

He knew he'd given her reason to do far worse.

The moment she'd arrived in the warehouse, carrying a gun, quaking head to toe, and demanding to know why he'd killed her brother, he'd lost everything. He'd only just persuaded her to give him another chance, and he'd been the one she'd turned to after losing Damian.

Every bit of this is your fault, he reminded himself. *Every last piece of it.*

He stood between the desk and the operating table. Mia sat at the computer, her brown eyes narrowed and the glow the screen cast across her face eerie as she sifted through files and memories. Eddie had briefly mentioned second thoughts about what they were planning, and Mia had demanded to be the one to ensure that Lila's memories remained gone.

Lila lay on the table, pale and unconscious, electrodes connected to each of her temples. Her cheeks were tear-streaked. At the sight of her, Eddie's knees weakened.

He'd never anticipated seeing his first creation in such a vulnerable position. He'd never intended her any harm.

"Mia, I don't—"

"It's done," Mia said flatly. She pushed back from the desk, and her chair bobbed where it hovered a few inches from the floor as she stood. She strode past Eddie on her way toward the table, giving his shoulder a squeeze that was too tight for comfort. "Too late."

Eddie recalled the first time he'd lain on the operating table within LDE's lab. Damian had been beside him, smiling encouragingly with a glint of determination in his eyes and assuring Eddie the first scan would be painless.

"After that… we'll do our best to keep it that way."

Eddie swallowed. He nodded stiffly and reminded himself of why he'd volunteered for this. Mia, the android he'd designed to donate to the United States military to serve as a substitute for human soldiers in order to save lives, had inadvertently killed Damian's parents during a demonstration of her capabilities gone terribly wrong. The official report had said only that Henry and Samantha had been killed in a car accident in which a woman had run into the road and caused a van to swerve into their vehicle, but Eddie knew. He'd been there—he'd been watching her at West Point as she'd slaughtered the soldiers she'd been tasked with fighting, and when she'd fled the base, he'd followed her outside. But he'd been too late. By the time he'd reached her, the police had already been on the scene, and the parents of his two best friends and their sister had already been dead.

When Damian, distraught after the loss of his parents and searching for solace, had suggested the company use its technology to find ways to preserve human life after death, Eddie had volunteered to serve as the test subject.

"Ready when you are," he said with an attempt at a smile.

Damian secured the electrodes attached to either side of Eddie's head, and then he moved toward the computer, where Derek sat.

"Close your eyes and try to clear your mind," said Damian.

A jolt of pain shot through Eddie's temple, and he raised his hand to brush the area. The headaches had grown more frequent since the night at the warehouse when he'd been faced with the fallout of his actions. He'd been shot in the knee, and he reasoned that he must've hit his head when he'd fallen to the concrete floor. He could think of no other reason for the splitting pain that now came to him more than once a day.

"Are you all right?"

Eddie blinked and looked up into the thin, pointed face of Mia. Her cropped auburn hair fell to her chin, and her lips were set in a frown.

For an instant, an image of her face contorted with rage flashed through his mind.

"You want to shut me down?" her cool alto demanded in his mind. *"For her?"*

As quickly as the image had come, it evaporated, and he was left with only the concerned Mia staring at him and the place where Desi had been standing a moment earlier on the telesense. Derek still stood at the podium, but Eddie couldn't focus on his words.

The headline at the bottom of the screen now read *"Desdemona Lawrence Refuses to Acknowledge Relationship with Brother's Killer."*

"Fine," Eddie told Mia. "Just a headache."

Chapter Two

Stories beneath the balcony, the vertical layers of traffic barely twitched. Lila watched the rush hour commuters and listened to their agitated honks, and she found herself grateful that she only had to rely on cars if she chose to do so. She turned away from the sight at the sound of a knock, and she left the balcony and made her way to the door of the hotel room where she'd taken up residence. The room was largely decorated in golden hues, and Lila had taken time to make the bed and ensure that her dresser was spotless, her clothes put away out of sight.

She was still earning back Derek's favor whether he would acknowledge it or not, and she was determined to look like she had her life together in every way possible.

With a smile, she opened the door. He stood on the threshold on a t-shirt and jeans, and Lila's lips twitched as she realized how quickly he'd changed after the press conference.

"Glad you could make it," she said.

"Thanks for agreeing to help me," said Derek.

When he entered, Lila closed the door behind him and led him to the chair at her desk. She drew up another from the corner and sat beside him. Derek produced his phone and tapped the display, and a projection of a call log shot upward over the screen.

"Ryder found Damian's phone hidden in the warehouse when his people swept it." Derek reached into his pocket and withdrew another small silver phone. The screen was shattered so severely that several flecks of glass were missing and anything projected would be unintelligible. "I think it was in his pocket when he... when he tried to run. I had all its information backed up and offloaded onto mine. Look at this."

He flicked the display and scrolled to July twenty-fifth, where an outgoing call at 6:13 P.M. indicated that Damian had spoken with Eddie for less than two minutes. This was followed by another at 10:49 that had lasted thirty-four seconds and a third at 11:02 that hadn't been answered.

"He was determined to talk to Eddie," said Lila. "Judging by how close together the last two were, I'd say he was worried about something."

Derek nodded. "And look at this." He closed the log and tabbed over to Damian's emails. He clicked a message labeled "Urgent."

Mr. Lawrence:

We have tried again to contact your business partner regarding Mia, and we have received no response. We believe she could be a danger to him, to you, and to those close to you. The Division will send someone to speak with you personally within the coming days and ensure your safety, and we will be reaching out to your brother, as well.

K. Seward

Lila blinked. "What the hell?" she muttered. "Damian knew about Mia?"

"Desi said Eddie brought up something about a creation of his when she followed him to the warehouse, like Mia had something to do with why he went after Damian. I looked through the rest of his messages and couldn't find any other correspondence with this person." His tone grew harder. "Either my brother deleted it or someone else did."

"Is there any way we can access Eddie's files through LDE?" Lila asked. "To find out who 'K. Seward' is? And the 'Division'?" As soon as the words had left her lips, she felt simulated heat rushing to her cheeks. She knew what she'd suggested was an invasion of privacy, and though it was nowhere near as dire as that through which Eddie had entered her mind and reprogramed her, she couldn't deny feeling guilty for proposing it.

Derek paused, his brow furrowing thoughtfully.

"I'll talk to Andrew in security tomorrow and see what he can dig up," he said at last. After a beat, he spoke again. "Do you want to come with me?"

Lila's stomach fluttered. "I'd love to."

He's starting to trust me again, she assured herself. *If nothing else, that much is progress.*

As Horus slept, Hathor studied his face. It was only subtly lined, and those lines would never grow deeper, as he had been created to resemble a man in his late twenties to early thirties. His nose and chin were long and sharp, and his hair was a close-cropped coppery brown. Though his eyes were closed, Hathor knew that if she could see them, his irises would be the same bright emerald as her own.

They had been made together and made to remain that way. Their creators had named them for gods and patterned their personalities after their namesakes, but Hathor clung to the fact that though she had been programmed to love Horus, she hadn't truly allowed herself to do so until they had escaped death together several times. When the Division had turned on its creations and sent assassins to eliminate them, the man assigned to target Horus had been foolish enough to do so when Hathor had been with him. She'd taken care of the problem and left the assassin's body on West Point's lawn as a message to the Division that she would not stand for their betrayal.

She'd been more than happy to do everything required of her thus far to ensure that Osiris's plan to exact vengeance on their creators was successful.

Quietly and carefully, Hathor slid out from beneath the satin sheets and pulled on the thin red dress she'd left on the floor beside the bed. She opened the door and crept out of the room. She hadn't always had trouble sleeping, but over the last few weeks, since their plans had begun their motion in earnest, her mind had been far too active at night to allow her peaceful rest.

She padded down the hallway and into the living room, and at the sight of Eddie sitting on the sofa, a book open in his lap, she paused, arching a brow.

"Can't sleep?" she asked.

He shook his head and stretched, and she couldn't miss the dark circles beneath his eyes.

"Seems I'm not the only one," he said.

"What's keeping you up?"

Hathor made her way toward the sofa and sat down, drawing her legs up beneath her as she watched Eddie. He closed his book and laid it on the end table beside him.

"Headaches," he said. "And I've just felt… off, recently. I don't know if it's stress or if it's—"

"Guilt?" Hathor offered. The moment after she'd spoken, she bit her inner cheek, inwardly chastising herself for being flippant. Her interactions with humans had been severely limited, and she was never certain how to handle them.

Eddie sighed. "I suppose."

The words bubbled up within Hathor so rapidly that she only had an instant to debate whether she should let them out, and her curiosity won over her tact.

"Then why did you do it?"

Eddie said nothing immediately. He studied his hand where it sat on the sofa's arm. Hathor held perfectly still, afraid that she might scare him off if she were to speak again or move too quickly.

"I didn't feel like I had a choice," he said at last. "Someone at the Division had contacted Damian about Mia, and I felt like the world was crashing down around me. Like everything I'd spent decades working for was about to be ripped away, and I couldn't do anything other than watch it all burn. I don't know if they told him that Mia killed his parents. I never asked. But if he knew… I never would've stopped paying for that. And the best part is I know I never will, even now. Every day, I regret the things Mia's done. But I don't regret her. I never responded to Hartley or her people after the last trial. I know they think she's too dangerous, and I don't want her destroyed."

As he spoke, the tense knot in Hathor's stomach eased. She'd had her doubts about whether it was wise to keep Eddie here in her home, but now that she knew for certain that he was loyal to Mia, she could allow her worries to fade.

"She thinks you hung the moon," said Hathor quietly.

Eddie shook his head. "That's probably very unwise."

Hathor inhaled. "Well, be that as it may, it's true." She stood and stretched. "I hope you manage to get some rest."

"Same to you."

She glanced over her shoulder to give him a small smile on her way back toward her room, and as she did so, she caught sight of a flash of auburn from the doorway that led to the kitchen.

Desi smoothed her black skirt over her knees, doing her best to ignore the pounding of her heart. She sat in front of a desk adorned with stacks of holofiles and a silver placard that read "Bennet E. McNaire, Attorney at Law" in sharp, bold letters. The window behind the desk gave way to a skyscraper across the street, and for an instant, Desi wondered whether Ben ever tired of being unable to see the sky from here. She glanced up to find her grey-suited attorney retrieving a notepad and pen from one of his desk's drawers, and then he sat across from her, watching her with polite interest.

She'd had sparing contact with Ben McNaire since the warehouse, but today was the first time he'd called her to insist that she meet him as soon as possible. She'd tried her best not to think about what that could mean on the way to his firm on the other side of Manhattan.

"Thank you for coming to see me on such short notice," he said.

Desi studied him. His blond hair was cut close to his head, and the set of his lips was pensive but unthreatening. The knot Desi's stomach had wound itself into loosened a little as she allowed herself to hope this meant she wasn't in immediate danger of arrest.

"I was worried," she admitted. "Is something wrong?"

Ben inhaled and rolled his shoulders backward, pulling a pair of holographic newspapers from a drawer to his right and laying them on the desk in front of her.

The words "Dodson Taking the Rap for Lawrence Sister?" glared up at her in large black script from the headline projected just above the paper on the left, and the one on the right read "Lawrence-Dodson Scandal?"

Desi gripped the arms of her chair in an attempt to steady herself.

"Jesus," she muttered.

"Do you think there's any way the police could come at you with accusations like this?"

She swallowed hard. "They know better," she said.

Ben raised a brow. "Forgive me, but that doesn't seem like them. In my experience, in a murder case, they interrogate everyone who could've possibly been involved—that's not to say I think you were, not at all, I—" He lowered his head and let out a heavy sigh. "What I mean to say is that if you feel like you might be in danger of being interrogated, I would be more than happy to represent you specifically."

Desi's pulse accelerated. She hadn't begun to consider that she could actually be connected with the crime outside of media speculation and efforts to smear her. But was it a possibility?

"Captain Ryder is aware of a few things we haven't given official statements on," she said carefully. An image of

Mia lifting Eddie from the warehouse floor flicked through her mind, and she closed her eyes as though doing so would make it disappear. In reality, the darkness only made the image clearer. She opened her eyes again to find Ben watching her with an arched blond brow.

"Are you okay?" he asked. "Would you like a glass of water?"

"I'm fine, thank you," said Desi with a small shake of her head. "I just mean that even if someone tried to start an investigation like that, I don't think it would get very far. The captain knows enough to be certain that I had nothing to do with it."

"I see." Ben glanced down at the headlines and then returned his focus to Desi. "If at any point you feel like passing that information on to me, I could prepare to combat this from all angles. I know you're wary of getting the media too involved, but if there's anything that would help keep your name clear, then I would—"

"Thanks," said Desi evenly. "I appreciate that very much, and I'll be sure you're the first person I tell, if it becomes necessary."

"Thank you," said Ben. "And if you need anything at all, please don't hesitate to reach out." He leaned forward just slightly in his seat, and Desi gathered that he was speaking less as an attorney than a confidante. "I can't imagine how much stress you're under, especially now, with your promotion. Congrats, by the way."

He smiled, and the expression lit up his face. Desi did her best not to dwell on how handsome his smile was.

"Thank you," she said.

She felt a buzz from within the purse leaning against her side, and she reached on instinct for her phone, sliding it up within her purse just enough to read the message from Derek that had appeared on her screen.

There's a situation. Get to LDE ASAP, please. Security room.

Desi frowned. She looked up at Ben, whose smile had faltered slightly.

"I'm sorry, I have to go. My brother needs me at LDE."

"No, no, I understand. Thank you for coming by."

Ben held out a hand, and he gripped Desi's warmly when she took it.

"I promise I'll keep you updated," she said. She stood, straightened her skirt, and moved for the door.

Please don't let anyone be hurt this time.

"Is there anything else you'd like to add, Miss Mitchell?"

Ravenna shook her head, working to keep her expression perfectly neutral. She stood across the breakfast bar from Detective Harry Masters, who hovered in one of the royal-blue-upholstered barstools Damian had picked out for his birthday only two months earlier. His hair was light brown, and he wore a black coat that trailed over the back of his stool.

"Let me read this back to you, then," said Detective Masters.

He swiped downward on the display projected over his phone, and his keyboard vanished, leaving only his notes. Ravenna glanced over the text, which was projected backward from where she sat, and bit back a sigh.

"So you were contacted by Derek Lawrence and the android Lila, who suspected Edward Dodson was involved in the death of Damian Lawrence."

"Yes," said Ravenna evenly.

"And they reached out to you because you were—"

"Damian's fiancée."

"And they considered that sufficient justification to endanger you because you're 'trained in self-defense.'"

"I am." Ravenna nodded and folded her hands on the white marble of the bar, focusing on the cool stone and not on the heat of the agitation rising within her.

"And at the LDE warehouse, you fired on Dodson."

Ravenna's jaw clenched. "Yes. Defending Desi. He did have a gun to her head."

Masters studied her, his index finger hovering a millimeter above his screen, and then gave her a stiff nod.

"All right. I'll be in touch if my department has any follow-up questions. Thank you for your time, Miss Mitchell."

Masters stood, and Ravenna led him to the front door without another word. She closed the door behind him when he'd gone and rested her forehead against it.

She couldn't believe Damian had had the foresight to leave her their home in his will. No matter how the NYPD tried to find ulterior motives for her presence here or her role in the warehouse's siege, she was protected, at least in terms of retaining her home.

A knock on the other side of the door sent a low, vibrating thrum through Ravenna's skull, and she frowned.

"Forget something, Detective?" she called flatly.

"It's us, Rae."

At the sound of Desi's voice, Ravenna pulled open the door to find her friend looking pale, her eyes ringed with dark circles. Beside Desi stood Derek, whose mouth was set in savage determination. Lila was behind them, offering Ravenna a small smile and glancing every few seconds to a dark-haired African American man Ravenna didn't recognize. He wore a white button-down shirt, and his mouth was set apprehensively.

"What is it?" Ravenna asked.

She stepped backward to allow the group room to enter, and she glanced down the empty path behind them, confirming that Masters was nowhere in sight before closing the door.

"We've found something you need to see," said Derek.

"And you didn't think calling first was logical?"

"It's important," said Desi firmly. "You need to see it in person."

Ravenna waved the group forward and led them to the living room, gesturing them to the sofa as she settled into a plush navy chair. Lila sat at one end of the sofa, perched on its edge as though she were prepared to fly away at any moment, and Desi stood by the dormant fireplace, staring into its depths with a distance in her eyes that Ravenna couldn't identify. She supposed whatever they had come to show her had something to do with Eddie.

Derek, on the other hand, crossed the room and stood beside the telesense.

"Can you project it up here, Andrew?" he asked the man Ravenna didn't recognize.

"Yes, sir."

Andrew produced a silver phone and projected its display to the telesense, all the while doing a fair job of hiding his apprehension, though Ravenna could still see it lurking in his eyes. On the telesense was what looked like a phone's home screen with LDE's logo as its wallpaper.

"I've had Damian's records backed up so that I can try to figure out why Eddie went after him."

Ravenna's fingers tightened on her knee.

"And what did you find?" she asked.

"Correspondence from someone named Seward, who said she's part of something called the 'Division.' I asked Andrew to help me pull some of Eddie's records from LDE's database to see if he had any info on Mia stored there or anything on where they might be. Andrew, please."

She watched the screen as Andrew clicked on the phone's email icon, and the image shifted to a message that had already been pulled up.

Mr. Dodson:

I received your message regarding Mia's completion. The Division is highly interested in her progress and wishes to see her. Please respond with your availability in the next month to come to our base of operations and allow us to test her.

Yours sincerely,

Clarisse Mitchell

"That's the first of several messages between Eddie and this 'Clarisse'."

Ravenna barely heard Derek's words; she was too busy staring at the name at the bottom of the screen, and she was certain she'd gone pale.

"I know it's a longshot and it's probably a decently common name, but didn't you have an aunt named Clarisse who worked in Washington?"

Ravenna swallowed. She tore her eyes from the screen at last to survey the people seated around her, and she tried her hardest not to sigh. Derek was watching her expectantly, and Lila was watching her, as well, though she seemed almost apologetic and glanced to the floor every few seconds. Desi was staring blankly into the dark fireplace, and Andrew was fidgeting on his feet.

"Yes," Ravenna said at last.

"And could this be her?" Derek pressed. There was a wild quality to his eyes Ravenna had never seen in him. She recognized it, though, as something she'd seen in many of her fellow assassins over her years of tracking and killing for money and what she'd always considered justice. Derek was on a hunt—for Eddie, for Mia, or simply for answers, she didn't know—and he wouldn't relent until he had completed it.

Ravenna recalled the rumors that had stalked her aunt when Clarisse had been working for President Hartley, and she knew she couldn't entirely deny the possibility.

"It might be," she said. "I haven't spoken to her in fourteen years. I doubt she'd want to tell me if she was somehow involved in creating that android bitch. No offense." Ravenna inclined her head to Lila, who gave a stiff shrug.

"I'm nothing like her," Lila muttered.

Are you sure? You've both killed.

Ravenna silenced these thoughts as quickly as they had come. She reminded herself that she didn't—she couldn't—blame Lila for what had happened to Damian. She'd forgiven her already, and even though anger slipped back through the cracks of her mind now and then for the man she'd loved and the life she'd lost, she would not give in to it.

After all, as she reminded herself more often than she would ever admit aloud, she hadn't lost every piece of that life. She knew she would have to tell the others of her pregnancy sooner or later, but at the moment, later seemed like the vastly more appealing option.

"Do you know where she lives?" asked Derek.

"Last I heard, Highland Falls."

"That's only about fifty miles from here," said Lila.

Ravenna inhaled. "We could go and see."

"Would you mind keeping an eye on LDE while we see this through?" Derek asked Desi. She blinked and seemed to refocus on the people surrounding her, and she nodded.

"I can do that," she said.

"Thank you." Derek looked to Andrew. "Are all of those files copied onto my phone?"

"Yes, Mr. Lawrence. And I'm not entirely sure I should be here. Doesn't this seem like something for the cops to handle?"

"As long as you don't tell the media about all this, I don't mind if you know," said Derek.

 Andrew nodded and said nothing further.

"When are you wanting to leave?" asked Ravenna.

"As soon as possible," said Derek.

Ravenna rolled her shoulders backward and pushed herself to her feet. "First thing in the morning, then."

Chapter Three

"We've lost three agents so far, and there are still at least four who haven't checked in for more than a day. And our trackers are still offline."

Rachel pinched the bridge of her nose and pulled in a deep breath. She knew if she opened her eyes, she would find Abigail Knight still pacing the area in front of her desk, and she knew the sight would only add more stress to the deluge she'd already been feeling.

"Do we have any other way of locating the androids?" she asked. "Can we hack into them somehow?"

"They weren't designed that way. From what I can gather, your mother and Clarisse didn't want enemies to be able to get into their heads, and they managed to lock us out, too."

Rachel opened her eyes at last. As she'd imagined, Abigail was pacing the carpet, her arms folded and her tan-painted lips pursed.

"We need to tell McNaire," said Rachel.

At this, Abigail froze, blinking before rounding on where Rachel sat.

"Ma'am, do you really think that's wise?"

"I don't want to deal with him any more than you do, but we need a protective detail on him until we can be sure the threat is neutralized."

A sharp pain bloomed across Rachel's temple, and she was fairly certain the thought of facing President Ethan McNaire had caused it. She'd sworn to herself that she would never enter his office again without someone she trusted there to hold her back if she finally snapped and retaliated against one of his snide comments about her mother.

"Do you want to go to Washington," Abigail began, "or do you want me t—?"

A high-pitched ringing interrupted her words, and Rachel looked down at the phone sitting on her desk. The screen projecting "Kat" just above it.

"One moment, please," Rachel said quickly. "She's on assignment."

Which means this can't be good.

Rachel tapped the *"Answer"* button followed by *"Speaker."*

"What's going on, Kat?" she asked.

"Mia's tailing us." Kat's voice was breathy, as though she'd been running.

"What?" Rachel demanded. Her stomach dropped as she locked eyes with Abigail, whose composure slipped for an instant to give way to a panic she quickly squashed again.

"Where are you?" Rachel asked her cousin, looking down at the phone.

"Queens," said Kat. "We're making sure we've lost her, and then we're moving forward with the plan for an ambush. I don't know how successful it will be, given the circumstances, but we need to scope out Dodson's place, and with any luck, she'll go back there when she's lost us."

"All right," said Rachel. Just be careful."

"Aren't we always?"

The line went dead.

Rachel inhaled. "That's all for right now, Abigail. I'll call you when I know more."

"Yes, ma'am." Abigail nodded. She turned on her heel and left the office, closing the door behind her.

When she'd gone, Rachel lowered her head into her hands.

Why the hell does nothing work the way we plan?

Within seconds, her phone rang again, its screen projecting *"Andrew."*

Rachel answered it on the first ring, holding it to her ear this time instead of putting the call on speaker.

"Andrew."

"We have a problem."

Rachel tensed, her grip tightening on her phone.

"What kind?" she asked carefully.

"The Lawrences and Lila know about the Division."

Rachel felt as though the floor had dropped out from beneath her, and the room was spinning. She closed her eyes once more.

"What?" she demanded.

"My cover is in their security department, Rachel. I couldn't exactly tell Derek no when he asked me to get into Dodson's files so he could figure out why Damian had a message from 'K. Seward' about Mia."

Slowly, Rachel leaned forward and rested her forehead on her desk. She couldn't believe the caution they had employed for years to keep LDE's other executives from learning about Dodson's work for the Division had been useless.

"And what's worse," Andrew continued, "they told Ravenna Mitchell. She's taking them to Clarisse as we speak."

Rachel imagined McNaire sitting in his office, a glass of whiskey in his hand as he laughed at how thoroughly her plans had collapsed all at once. She supposed it was fortunate, at the very least, that she hadn't had this information to give Abigail.

"Come back to base," she told Andrew. "There's no point in maintaining your post."

"I'm sorry," said Andrew. "You have no idea how sorry I am."

"It's not your fault. Just get here so we can figure out what to do."

★

Ravenna took a sip from her water glass, observing Derek and Lila over its rim.

They sat across the table from her at the deli where they had stopped for an early lunch, talking animatedly and watching each other with far too much interest and affection to be platonic. As far as she knew, neither of them had said anything to the other on the matter of their strange relationship, but she had always been an astute observer, and try as she might, she couldn't ignore the feeling of discomfort that crept up through her stomach as she watched them.

With a small sigh, she replaced her glass on the table.

Don't be jealous. It's not their fault.

She wondered if she would ever be able to move on. To stop hurting over Damian and resenting the world for continuing to spin without him.

"Are you okay?"

Ravenna blinked. It took a moment for her to process that she was the one Lila had addressed. She looked up, met Lila's eyes, and nodded.

"Yeah, I'm fine."

Lila looked unconvinced but didn't press the matter further. "What do you think your aunt has to do with Eddie and Mia?" she asked instead.

Ravenna frowned. Try as she might, she couldn't make the pieces fit together. "I don't know," she answered honestly. "She was President Hartley's Senior Advisor, and I used to visit her in Washington during the summer when I was in school. The only thing I ever remember being out of the ordinary was the time they dragged us off to West Point."

As the waitress appeared and began refilling everyone's glasses, Ravenna allowed herself to slip back to the first time she'd met Isabella Hartley.

"Feet off the desk."

Ravenna groaned. "C'mon, Aunt Clarisse. It's not like I'm hurting anything."

"Feet off, Ravenna."

With a long, drawn-out sigh, Ravenna obliged. She pulled her feet off the desk and returned them to the floor in front of her, crossing her ankles and drumming her fingers impatiently on the sides of the chair she occupied in front of President Hartley's desk in the Oval Office. She twisted around in the chair to face her aunt, who stood at the rear of the room.

"Okay. They're off."

"*Don't be like that,*" said Clarisse. She resembled Ravenna strongly, with the same dark hair and pale complexion, and she was in her mid-thirties. "*Be glad you're here at all. How many of your friends can say that they've been to the Wh—*"

"*…The White House, or that they have an aunt who works for the president? None. I know. I understand. Thank you for bringing me, and all that. But I really don't think that putting my feet on the desk is a breach of national security.*" She rolled her eyes. Ravenna was thirteen, and while she appreciated being asked to spend a few weeks of her summer with her aunt in Washington, D.C., she didn't enjoy all the rules and restrictions that applied to her aunt's workplace, even if said workplace was the White House.

"*Rae, I don't think even Isabella does that. You just… don't. It's the Oval Office. That should be respected.*"

Ravenna sighed and stood, moving across the room to lean against the wall. She hadn't dared to touch the president's chair, and she'd thought the momentary indulgence of propping her feet on the desk from the additional chair on its other side would be received as a joke.

"*So what are we waiting on, anyway?*" she asked.

"*She needs to speak with me,*" said Clarisse. "*I don't know how she's going to react to you being here, but I don't really have another option, unless you're somehow able to pull a license out of thin air and drive yourself back to my house.*"

"*No, not exactly. What does she need to talk to you about?*"

"*Well… I don't know how much I'm allowed to tell you.*"

"*Ooh, classified.*" Ravenna grinned.

"*Yeah. Sorry. I wish I could tell you, but we're waiting until we're certain that what we're trying to do is actually possible.*"

"*I think that time has come.*"

Ravenna jumped and looked toward the voice. In the doorway stood President Hartley. She wore a navy blazer and knee-length black skirt, and her red hair was pulled into a tight bun behind her head.

"*Madam President,*" *Clarisse greeted her respectfully.*

Ravenna blinked. In the many visits she'd paid to her aunt over the years, she had never come this close to the president. Ravenna was not accustomed to finding herself at a loss for words, but at that moment, she was speechless. She blanched as Hartley turned to her, offering a hand.

"*You must be Ravenna,*" *said the elder woman, smiling.*

With a nod, Ravenna took Hartley's hand gingerly and shook it.

"*Clarisse talks about you all the time.*" *Hartley smiled, glancing from Ravenna to her aunt and back again.* "*I hope you're enjoying your time here.*"

"*It's... an honor to meet you, ma'am.*" *Ravenna attempted to keep her voice steady despite the nerves that were getting the better of her.* "*I... definitely. I need to remember to keep my feet off the furniture, though.*" *She let out an anxious laugh, which the others returned, Clarisse with admonishment and Hartley with warmth.*

"*Probably not a bad idea,*" *said Clarisse.*

"*Oh, it's all right. Just don't let anyone catch you.*" *Hartley winked.*

Ravenna smiled gratefully. She then turned to her aunt, raising her eyebrows and allowing her smile to shift into a smirk. "*See? Told you.*"

"*Yes, I see.*" *Clarisse gave her a thin smile.*

"*They've finished, Clarisse,*" *said Hartley, her formal tone returning.*

Clarisse's eyes widened. Ravenna frowned, searching her aunt's face for answers, but she found none.

"*We need to fly north to see what they've done. I know this was supposed to be your time off from all of it, but I've just been told that they need you, me, and everyone else involved to come as quickly as possible.*"

Clarisse nodded. "Of course. But what about Ravenna?"

"*She can wait with Rachel. If she's all right with that, of course.*"

"*That's… definitely fine with me,*" *spluttered Ravenna.* I don't have a clue what they're talking about, *she thought,* but I know who Rachel is. I wonder if she knows anything about what's going on with—

"*Okay. Let's go, then.*" *Hartley turned for the door, with Clarisse and Ravenna in tow. When they reached the hallway outside, Secret Service officers fell in at their sides and guided them out of the building and to the tarmac where Air Force One waited. The plane was white with a blue stripe running down its side, and it was larger than Ravenna had anticipated. Her stomach fluttered with excitement at the sight of it, and she paused. She withdrew her phone and quickly snapped a photo before being ushered aboard by her aunt. She silently took the seat she was directed to beside a redheaded girl she instantly recognized as the First Daughter.*

Rachel Hartley looked like a miniature version of her mother, down to the blazer and the thoughtful expression she wore. Evidently sensing that she was no longer alone, Rachel turned away from the window she had been staring out of and looked up with a simple "Hello."

Though the President's daughter was one year her junior, Ravenna felt a sort of reverence toward this girl that was known the world over. She smiled.

"Hi. I'm Ravenna."

"Rachel." She returned Ravenna's smile and extended a hand, which Ravenna shook.

"I know." Ravenna's cheeks burned. Couldn't you have come up with something smarter than that? *she mentally screamed at herself. "Clarisse is my aunt," she added quickly.*

Rachel nodded. "So you're coming with us?"

"I guess so. Where are we going, anyway?"

Rachel paused. She glanced over Ravenna's shoulder before leaning conspiratorially toward her. "West Point, New York."

Ravenna raised a brow. "Why?"

"I'm not really sure," said Rachel with a shrug. "They won't talk about it when I'm around. I guess it's some big secret."

"Your food should be out shortly," said the waitress. She turned and walked away to assist another group of people.

"Did your aunt say anything about androids?" asked Lila.

"Not… directly."

"Don't be modest," said Derek, cracking a smile. "Ravenna gave us the idea that led to LDE after a trip to the White House."

Lila's blue eyes widened. "Really?"

Ravenna shrugged. "Sort of. I… 'accidentally' grabbed one of the files from Aunt Clarisse's desk one day."

The others laughed, and, despite herself, Ravenna couldn't hold back a grin.

"What? I was young. I was curious. I was… a breach of national security, actually. She never found out, though." Ravenna paused. "Not that I know of, at least. Anyway, the file said something about androids. How they could be beneficial to society, do jobs people might find too dangerous, and things like that. I didn't get to read much of it; I heard my aunt coming and had to put it back before she realized I was reading it. But I said something about it to Damian, and he was… intrigued."

"Wow. Well… thank you," said Lila. "I wouldn't be here without you."

Ravenna smiled again but said nothing. While she had begun again to consider Lila her friend, a small, selfish part of her also realized that if LDE had never begun, Eddie would have never been able to use Lila as a murder weapon.

Damian would still be alive.

Chapter Four

"...and with figures like these, our net profit from last year will triple. Easily. The media coverage is blasting our android sales through the roof."

Glad someone's benefitting from this circus, thought Desi, fighting to keep her expression neutral. She sat at the head of the long table in LDE's main conference room, and men and women in suits surrounded her, speaking in terms she had been trying all morning to get accustomed to hearing. Her muscles buzzed and ached to get up and move, and the clock on the rear wall told her it was 11:35.

"Would you like something else, Miss Lawrence?"

Desi looked up at Dana, the android patterned after Lila who served as the personal assistant to the company's co-presidents when LDE was in full operation. Dana was a later model, designed at least a decade after Lila, and though her facial structure was similar, she looked closer to Lila's sister than anything else. Her jaw was a bit squarer, her nose smaller, and her complexion was closer to tan than Lila's pallor. Her hair was light brown. Desi had never had much interaction with Dana in the past, but she was comforted by her presence. She didn't know any of the other executives in the room, and having at least one familiar face eased her mind slightly.

"Another cappuccino, please, Dana," she said. She'd already drained three cups since her arrival at eight, and she knew she would pay for her caffeine addiction later, but she couldn't bring herself to care right now. She found staying awake with coffee until she crashed vastly preferable to the nightmares she hadn't been able to escape since the warehouse, and if coffee would keep her awake enough to pay at least some attention to this board meeting, she would gladly face the consequences.

"Right away, ma'am." Dana nodded and followed the long, thin table to the door at its other side, and she started down the hallway. Desi wanted nothing more than to follow her and abandon the meeting, but she knew that wasn't an option.

"...and with your blessing, Miss Lawrence, our research and development branch would like to begin work on a prototype for the LA-760."

A cursory glance around the room told Desi that all eyes were fixed on her, and she inhaled.

"Tell me more about it, please," she said.

The balding man sitting halfway down the table to her left nodded. "She's the newest variation of the Lila model, and she's a response to public worry regarding hacking. After..." The man trailed off, seemed to rethink where his words had been headed, and tried again. "People are worried that their products might not be entirely secure. The new model has a series of failsafe mechanisms designed to keep outside influences at bay."

Desi resisted the cynical smile that threatened the edges of her lips. She supposed her brothers had never considered this type of failsafe necessary in the past, but she couldn't ignore the irony of its development after the problem had already presented itself.

"Go ahead with the prototype," she said. "It seems like a good direction to move in."

She glanced at the clock again, and at last, her restlessness got the better of her.

"Why don't we take a five-minute break and then reconvene?" she asked. "I think we could all use a stretch."

Murmurs of agreement passed around the table, and Desi pushed her hovering chair backward and got to her feet. She strode quickly into the hallway and around the nearest corner, where she leaned back against the wall and forced in a series of deep breaths.

"You can do this," she muttered. "You can."

She caught sight of her reflection in the glass door leading to Dana's office, and her breath caught in her throat. She'd never imagined herself the type for business suits, but she could almost be fooled into thinking she looked the part. She'd opted for neutral shades in her makeup, and the grey suit she wore was far more muted than her typical wardrobe.

Maybe if I fake it long enough, I'll become one of them.

"Desi?"

She looked up at the sound of the voice, and she spotted Ben approaching from the other end of the corridor. He grinned at her and made his way to her side.

"How's your first day?" he asked.

"I haven't set the place on fire, yet, so I guess that's something."

Ben chuckled. "It's better than I would've done. I was never good at this type of business. I interned at Hover in college, and it was a nightmare. Then again, I was mostly on coffee duty, so that could be why."

Desi tried to imagine the outgoing, well-spoken Ben being limited to fetching drinks and standing in the corner while other people worked, and she had to smile at the image's absurdity.

"I'm sure we could find you a job here doing that, if you'd like."

"I don't think so," he said, "but thank you. I did want to talk to you about work, though."

"Always business," Desi teased.

"Well, only halfway. I've drawn up some papers for you and your brother, including an order of protection against Dodson. I wondered if you might want to discuss all of it over lunch."

Desi blinked, and her heart missed a beat.

"I figured you might need break from the thrilling world of business," Ben continued.

"That actually sounds great. I can call you after the meeting ends. It can't be much longer, can it?" Desi asked hopefully. She knew the company hadn't had much of an opportunity to pull itself back together since July twenty-fifth, but she hadn't anticipated the series of consecutive meetings she'd been trapped in to last quite so long.

"I'd imagine it'll be over before you know it. Just give me a call when you're ready." Ben smiled at her and started off down the hall, and a moment later, Dana emerged from her office with a cappuccino, which she passed to Desi.

"Thank you," Desi muttered, still staring at the spot where Ben had disappeared.

Eddie stared unblinkingly at the perfect replica of himself.

This is wrong.

He examined the short, dark hair and grey eyes he'd seen in the mirror all his life reflected back at him in the form of the android copy he'd agreed to allow.

Eddie remembered the moment that Damian, turned away to stare out the window of his office with his hands braced on the sill, had suggested they use their work to find a way to preserve human life after death. Eddie had allowed his guilt to drive him to participate in the invasive procedure to copy his memories, his mannerisms, his entire personality into this duplicate body.

I want it decommissioned and hidden in the warehouse. I don't want anyone to know we did this.

If the experiment could keep someone from losing all of a loved one to death, he'd believed it was worth it.

As the duplicate blinked and pulled in a breath, Eddie questioned whether that was true.

"Goodnight. Lights."

As the living room went dark, Eddie was left with his thoughts and the ghost of Desi's kiss that still tingled on his lips. She'd been the one to make the move, this time, before she'd pulled back eventually and retreated to her bedroom. She'd insisted, though, that he stay on her couch instead of going home, and he took that as a good sign.

Perhaps she was starting to realize how strong the pull between them remained.

"Eddie?"

Mia's worried voice as she gently shook his shoulder pulled him back into the present. He blinked away the memory of Desi's apartment, and he found that the headache that had accompanied the series of images had disappeared as quickly as it had come. He turned away from the window in his borrowed bedroom and looked up to find Mia standing beside him. Her expression was neutral. Unreadable.

"I knocked. When you didn't answer, I came in. You were just staring out the window, not moving, not reacting." She paused. "It happened again, didn't it?"

"Yes."

"What was it this time?"

"It's... not important." His memories of Desi were the only solace he had now that he'd lost her—lost everyone and everything other than Mia. And Hathor, he supposed. He barely knew her, but she at least seemed willing to talk with him while he was living in isolation. Caged. "What's happening to me? I thought you said this was the worst of what they left me with."

He nodded to his leg, where the singed muscles still snagged and burned when he walked, though he could at least use the limb again.

"I don't know," Mia said with a shake of her head. "You fell three stories, Eddie. It's not a stretch to assume you hit something you shouldn't have."

"It's getting worse," he insisted. "The headaches make it hard to think, and I don't need to see my life repeated on a loop. I know how I got here."

Mia sighed. "I'll see if I can find a stronger medication. And I've been combing McNaire's files when he leaves the office. He's talking with Desdemona fairly often, and he's drawn up an order of protection against you."

Her words hit Eddie like a punch to the lungs. He pushed himself to his feet and gritted his teeth as pain ripped up his leg from the outside of his right knee.

"Does he think I'm going to go looking for her?" He let out a flat, humorless laugh.

"I think he just feels powerless," said Mia. She leaned back against the foot of the bed, her arms folded. "He's the Lawrence family lawyer, and he has no one to take to trial. And she hasn't told him about me, yet, that I've been able to find."

"Keep an eye on them. If it starts to look like he knows, give it up and stay away from him."

"Of course." Mia's tone was bored with these words, and she paused for a moment before speaking again with a bit more apparent interest. "I did find out something else. She's the only company head that's around. I don't know where Derek is, but Lila's gone, too, and so is Damian's fiancée."

Eddie frowned. "See if you can find them."

"I'll do what I can. But I have a few loose ends of my own to tie, too."

Eddie debated requesting an elaboration before deciding he really didn't want to know what she was planning, most likely with Osiris and the others.

"Be careful," he said.

She simply laughed, moving to the door in a flash and taking her leave.

"I don't think you know the meaning of the words," Eddie mumbled.

Derek glanced sideways at Lila as he maneuvered through the streets of Highland Falls. Her golden-blond hair was pulled back from her face, allowing him to see her eyes, which were a lighter blue than anyone else's that Derek had ever seen.

Lila happened to meet his gaze, and she smiled. He returned the gesture without pause.

He was beginning to worry.

He'd allowed himself to indulge the way he felt about her briefly when he'd persuaded himself to seek her out and protect her, but now that she was no longer in immediate danger, he'd tried his best to avoid any thoughts that might lead to acknowledging what he feared was true. He couldn't allow himself to love her.

Could he?

The morality of android-human relationships had been called into question before courts over the last few decades, but most of those courts had refused to pass judgments that could be considered legislation on the matter. The only case Derek knew of that had found a human at fault for filing a marriage certificate with an android had centered on an early Genesis model—an Eve, if he recalled correctly. The android's programming hadn't been sufficiently advanced for the court to rule that she held enough autonomy to make her own choices, at least not choices of that caliber. But Lila had been an advancement in technology the likes of which the world had never seen before her. She was, as the media had heralded her, "the world's first near-human android." Her thoughts were her own, her feelings were her own, and...

Derek realized he had no idea how she felt about him. He'd never asked her, and he had no idea whether it was wise to do so. If she didn't love him, would she have any desire to continue working with him, after he admitted something like that? Or would his admission strain their relationship to the point of breaking?

"It's the one on the right up here."

Ravenna's voice from the back seat pulled Derek rather abruptly into the present, and his focus flicked out the front windshield to the house in question.

It was small and off-white, with green shutters and a picket fence. Derek knew immediately that the house was old, as it wasn't made of metal, the way most buildings had been for the last century.

"You're sure?"

"Of course I am," said Ravenna impatiently.

Derek pulled the car up to the curb in front of the house and parked it. He, Lila, and Ravenna filed out and gathered on the passenger side, standing close together, each apparently waiting for one of the others to be the first to speak.

"After you," said Derek finally, looking at Ravenna.

She took a deep breath and gave a stiff nod, squaring her shoulders and striding to the gate at the center of the fence. She unhooked the latch, opened the gate, and led the way up the path to the house.

As he followed Ravenna toward the building, Derek felt something brush against his fingers. He looked down to see that it was Lila's hand, and electricity crackled up his arm at her touch. She gave his hand a quick squeeze, which he returned before she pulled out of reach.

Ravenna hesitated at the door.

"It'll be fine," Lila assured her. "She's your aunt. She'll tell you the truth."

"That's what I'm afraid of."

Ravenna knocked, and they waited in silence. Derek swallowed hard as he squared his shoulders.

There was a scuffling from within, followed by what sounded like footsteps nearing the group.

"Who is it?"

Ravenna cleared her throat. "Aunt Clarisse, it's me."

A small pause followed, and then the sound of a latch, and the door opened. The woman on the other side had dark brown hair that was greying at its roots, and her hazel eyes searched Derek and Lila warily. When her focus landed on Ravenna, her expression softened.

"They're my friends."

The woman Derek assumed to be Clarisse frowned slightly, glanced behind the group, and then addressed them. "Come in. Quickly."

They did as she bade them, stepping into the small sitting room at the front of the house. The room was cluttered, with books and newspapers and holofiles covering what space the green-and-white furniture did not.

Derek heard Clarisse close and lock the door behind them. She ushered them farther inside, waving them to the sofa. Somewhat uncertainly, Derek sat down, with Lila to his left and Ravenna on her other side. Clarisse sat across from them in an armchair.

"It's been so long," she said to Ravenna with an expression that suggested she still hadn't fully come to accept that her niece was actually sitting in the room with her. "Why now?"

"We need your help."

Derek turned to Ravenna, who looked somewhat guilty upon admitting that this was her reason for visiting.

Clarisse frowned. "What could I help you with? You're not in any sort of trouble, are you?"

"No, no," said Ravenna quickly. "It's not like that. We've come to talk to you about… the Division."

Clarisse blanched. She broke eye contact with Ravenna, looking instead down at her own folded hands in her lap.

"How do you know that name?"

Derek drew a deep breath. "It was mentioned in an e-mail you sent to Edward Dodson," he said. "Regarding the android Mia."

Clarisse continued to stare at her hands. "It's classified."

"Please, Aunt Clarisse. We need your help. It's urgent."

The elder Mitchell sighed. She looked up, and her eyes fell on Derek. "I know you. You're Derek Lawrence. And you—" She turned to Lila. "—you're the first LDE android."

Lila nodded slowly.

"To this day," said Clarisse, "we have no idea how they managed to perfect you. We tried so hard and for so long… We've lost so much."

Ravenna frowned. Derek exchanged a glance with Lila before returning his focus to Clarisse when she spoke again.

"It was during the Middle Eastern War. Human error caused so much pain and destruction. We needed a way to win the war, and our soldiers were dropping like flies. President Hartley had an idea—an idea that should have worked. We should have succeeded."

"So…" Lila hesitated. "Why didn't you?"

"What we were trying to do had never been attempted. We had no idea where to begin, when she told us to create the perfect soldier. One that would obey without question. An android."

Derek listened, both entranced and horrified. He couldn't imagine one of LDE's androids being turned into a soldier and ordered to kill on command.

A flash of Eddie suggesting they create a model for use by the military flashed through his mind, and he squashed it.

"The Division—the Perfect Soldier Division—was created to accomplish this. We assembled a team of the top minds in robotics at the time, hoping that, together, they could achieve the goal. Soon, a group of seven androids was created. They were exactly what we wanted: soldiers to the core. They fought perfectly in all our tests. We deployed them to take out a small band of enemy forces that had taken refuge in Dahab."

There was a long silence.

"What happened?" asked Lila.

"They couldn't find the enemy group. So… they tore the town apart. They killed everyone."

Lila gasped. Ravenna closed her eyes and sighed.

"My God," said Derek quietly.

"Needless to say," Clarisse plowed on, "the androids were decommissioned. We did our best to keep the situation quiet, but somehow the media got ahold of it, and our cover was almost blown. Several other Division officials and I decided to wait it out in Canada until the fever died down."

Ravenna dropped her head into her hands. "We believed you," she muttered.

"What was that?" asked Clarisse.

Ravenna looked up, her features set in a blend of disbelief and indignation. "We believed you when you said you had nothing to do with it. Mom, Dad, Bryce, me. We defended you to everyone—to our own family, to the reporters that came snooping. We lied to all of them. Bryce defended you until the day he died."

Clarisse's face fell. "Ravenna, I never meant for any of it to happen. I never wanted you to have to lie for me. But there was nothing I could do, I—"

"You could have told us." Ravenna stood, folding her arms across her chest. "We still would have lied to everyone else to protect you, but at least we would've known what was really going on."

"I couldn't," Clarisse said weakly. "I couldn't put you in danger like that."

"And look where we are now! Trying to figure out why you were working on something in secret with the man who killed my fiancé!"

There was silence. Clarisse turned her gaze to the floor.

"Ravenna, calm down," said Derek. "That's not going to get us anywhere."

She ignored him. "How did Eddie get involved?"

Clarisse sighed. "While we were out of the country, some of the scientists continued their research. They tried to fix the androids, to perfect them.   It never worked. Eventually, the others and I returned to the U.S. When the conflict with China began, the Division saw an opportunity to prove that they could finally succeed.   But they needed help. Your company was in the news all the time."   She inclined her head to Derek. "I recognized your names— yours, your brother's, and Edward's, I mean. I remembered hearing from Ravenna's father that she had friends interested in robotics when you were all in high school."

Derek shot Ravenna a look. Apparently, her aunt was unaware that she had inadvertently sparked that interest.

"We began… 'paying attention' to your company. We decided that of the three of you, Edward was the most likely to sympathize with our intentions. I approached him about designing something for the Division. We met again later, and he said he had run the idea by you and Damian."

Derek nodded vaguely. In the corner of his vision, he saw Lila tense.

"You didn't approve. However, Edward still wanted to help us. So he created Mia. She seemed like everything we'd hoped for. But… we were wrong. She had no conscience, no remorse. Like the androids the Division scientists creat- ed, she just destroyed. We tested her at our installation at West Point, and during her trial, four people were killed."

By this time, Derek was frowning deeply. It was not simply the revelation that Mia had killed that disturbed him, but that this had all occurred at West Point. Only a few blocks outside the Military Academy, his parents' fateful accident had taken place.

"Then she ran.   She left the building and took off through the streets. Derek, I…" Clarisse trailed off, but he didn't need to hear anything more. He already knew.

His lungs were on fire, and he couldn't stop the choked sound that burst from his throat.

Lila grabbed his hand. "What's wrong?"

Ravenna turned toward him, concern visible in her eyes. She glanced from him to her aunt and back again.

A long moment passed before he was able to speak. He squeezed Lila's hand tightly, hoping that holding onto her would lessen the pain.

"Mia killed my parents."

Chapter Five

Desi twisted a few lo mein noodles around her fork and slipped it into her mouth as she watched Ben across his desk. He took a bite of sesame chicken while poring over the documents laid out in front of him, and she had to admire his work ethic. She'd expected more off-topic conversation than actual progress on her family's case, and she was pleasantly surprised by how interested Ben seemed in helping her.

"Take a look at this right here," he said, sliding a holofile across the desk toward her. She shifted her takeout box to the side and leaned in to examine the file, which explained that if Eddie were to come within three hundred feet of her, she would have the right to inform the police. "This protects you if he even thinks about trying to approach you, and the clause below it is a no contact provision."

She ignored the twisting of her stomach at the thought. The Desi of two weeks earlier would have laughed at such a provision. The Desi who had sought comfort in Eddie's arms would have turned away and left the office, but the Desi who sat here today was wiser. She knew who Eddie really was, no matter what he had deceived her into thinking and feeling for him.

For an instant, she felt the brush of his fingers against her neck as he fastened the chain of a diamond solitaire around it, and a shiver rocked her body. She closed her eyes, inhaled, and released the breath.

Where did I put that damned thing, anyway?

When she opened her eyes, the room around her was silent. Ben watched her from the other side of the desk with a look of half-concealed panic.

"If I'm going too far by saying so," he began, "please tell me, and I'll stop. But I'm worried about you."

Desi shrugged with as much nonchalance as she could muster despite how cold her hands had become. She propped her fork against the side of her takeout box and folded her hands in her lap, clasping them in an attempt to warm them and trying not to acknowledge the quickening of her heart, which she could feel hammering against her ribs.

"There's really nothing to worry about," she said. "Though I appreciate it very much."

Ben sighed and ran a hand through his short blond hair.

"Did you see any doctors after... the incident at the warehouse?"

"Yes. They had to pull a bunch of glass shards out of me." Desi's tone was flatter than intended, and as she surveyed the portions of her arms that her three-quarter sleeves didn't cover, resentment bubbled within her. It wasn't directed at Ben but at Eddie, at Mia, at everyone who'd had a hand in her creation. She'd been told the thin white scars lining her arms, legs, and back would fade over time and that the doctors had done all they could without cosmetic surgery to make them disappear.

"I mean... have you talked to anyone about post-traumatic stress?"

Desi fixed her attention on the window behind Ben and the immense chrome building beyond it. She didn't think she could meet his eyes while discussing this.

"No, I haven't," she said. "I don't really have the time to worry about what's going on with me, right now. I have a company to run."

"Desi, that's not true. And it's not fair to you. I really think you should talk to someone about what you've been through. I can't imagine dealing with even half of it. The stress it would put on a person..."

"Really, Ben. Thank you, but I don't think I can do that right now."

Ben opened his mouth to respond, but at the sound of a knock on his office door, he looked past Desi and toward the sound.

"Yes?" he called.

"Detective Masters, Mr. McNaire. Could I have a word?"

Frowning, Ben met Desi's eyes once again. She shrugged.

"I can leave, if you like," she said.

"No, that's not necessary. Come in, Detective."

The door opened, and a man with fair hair and a long black coat entered.

"Ah, Miss Lawrence. It's a good thing you're here."

He crossed the room and laid his hands on the back of the chair beside the one Desi occupied, and then he spoke again.

"I was going to reach you through Mr. McNaire, but I guess it saves me the trouble."

"Reach her about what, Detective?" asked Ben with a raised brow.

Detective Masters let out a long breath. "I've been working your family's case, Miss Lawrence, and I have some troubling news. The security footage from the LDE warehouse has gone missing."

Desi's heart leapt into her throat, and she clutched the arm of her chair so tightly her knuckles went white. She looked from the detective to Ben, whose jaw tightened.

"What do you mean, it's gone missing?" Desi pressed, trying hard to keep the snap from her tone. She couldn't afford to make an enemy of a police officer, at the moment.

"It's gone, along with the footage from LDE itself. Its Manhattan headquarters, at least."

Desi leaned forward and lowered her head into her hands.

"And we're trying to narrow down our list of people who might've had reason to take it."

At this, Desi sat upright so quickly she might've been spurred by an electric current.

"You think I had anything to do with that?" she demanded.

"We have to cover all our bases, Miss Lawrence," said Masters, clasping his hands behind his back, "and considering that Dodson isn't exactly within our means to question, we're going to have to get information somehow."

"Are you charging my client with something?"

At the instantaneous switch that had flipped within Ben as his tone became cool and calculating, Desi scooted as far back in her chair as she could, all too aware of the new sense of danger that buzzed through the air. She knew she had nowhere to go and that if Masters wanted to charge her, Ben was her only line of defense. Still, she was so sickened by the thought of anyone trying to connect her to Damian's death that she wanted to run from the office and barricade herself in her apartment.

"No, sir," said Masters, shaking his head. "But I may have to talk with her over the next few days while we try to get this sorted out. Just procedure, you know. We have to talk to everyone who might know anything. And I've tried to get ahold of your brother," he added to Desi. "Is he out of town?"

"Yes. Family business," Desi lied.

"I see. Well, please tell him to return my calls, when he gets a chance. Enjoy your lunch."

Masters inclined his head to the takeout boxes on the desk and strode out the door.

When he'd gone, Desi allowed her rigid posture to deflate as she closed her eyes.

Just what we need, she thought. *Another damn complication.*

"Is everyone ready?" asked Kat. She glanced from one of her agents to the next as they nodded.

"As we'll ever be," said Charlie, whose tight, white-blond ponytail stood out like a flash bomb against her black clothing. Lex stood beside her at the group's center, and Casey was directly to Kat's right.

"All right," said Kat, "let's make this quick."

She started up the short path to the house from the street, beckoning the others after her and sticking to the shadows as much as possible. She ignored the yellow police tape warning her team against entry. She had no idea how long the NYPD would stay away. Unfortunately, though, they were the least of the Division's problems.

When Kat reached the door, she raised her Glock. She signaled to Charlie, who slid close and typed an access code into the panel beside the door. The light on the keypad turned from red to green, and Kat heard the door unlatch.

"Go," she ordered.

Charlie opened the door and held it until the others had entered. She closed it behind them and reactivated the security system from the inside panel.

"You all know what you're looking for," said Kat.

Without further instruction, they separated, each producing a flashlight to follow a predetermined path. Casey made her way up the stairs while Charlie sought out the basement. Lex followed the hall out of the foyer to the left, and Kat followed it to the right, flicking on her flashlight and examining the walls for doors.

The hallways were tall, the walls painted dark and the wood paneling along the top of each etched with leaves and vines. Kat's footsteps echoed across the hardwood floor, and she allowed herself for a moment to wonder exactly how old the home was. She rarely saw this sort of detailing, particularly in such a rare material.

She moved through the first door on her left and into a study. The beam from her flashlight fell on a vacant oaken desk and then a bookcase.

Of course the computer's gone, she thought. *He wouldn't make it that easy.*

She laid the flashlight sideways on the bookcase, and its glow illuminated most of the third shelf. Books were wedged tightly together, with holofiles interspersed between them. Kat immediately began sliding them out and examining them, hoping that something on the shelf would prove useful to her.

A sales report for LDE from last year. The complete works of Shakespeare. More sales reports. Business textbooks.

She shifted her flashlight down to the second shelf.

An atlas. A photo album. A… small black book with no title written on the side.

Kat lifted the small book with one hand and her flashlight with the other. As she flipped through the pages, endless handwritten notes flashed before her eyes.

…don't know what to do. If I follow through with what Clarisse wants, I'll be going against their wishes. Our work wouldn't be a weapon. It would be a way to improve human lives, to save them, and isn't that what we set out to do?

…started reading Othello. Will she laugh at me if I quote it to her? It didn't exactly play out well for the woman she's named after. I wonder what her name would've been if Samantha hadn't been a Shakespeare scholar.

…Feel different. Not quite normal. Not sure what's wrong with me. I remember talking to Mia in the warehouse and then… nothing. There's just empty space. Until a few hours later, at least. Something is wrong.

A scream pierced the night, followed by a succession of thuds. Kat jumped, whipping around and shining the flashlight out the door of the study. When she saw no one, she snapped the book shut and pulled it to her chest.

If the scream had come from within the house, she no longer had to worry about maintaining cover. She abandoned caution altogether.

"Lex! Charlie! Casey! Where are you?"

"Kat!"

At the sound of Casey's terrified shout, Kat darted out of the study and toward the foyer, doing her best to ignore the target her flashlight's wobbling beam painted on her head.

"What's happening?" she called as she entered the room. The instant her gaze landed on the staircase, however, any further words died in her throat.

Charlie lay in a heap at the foot of the stairs. Lex stood to her left, his pistol trained on something on the landing above them. Casey crouched on Charlie's right, taking her pulse at her neck.

Kat fell in between Lex and Casey, sliding the book behind her back.

At the top of the stairs stood a woman hidden in shadow.

"I don't believe you were invited here."

Hairs stood up along Kat's arms beneath her long black sleeves. She glanced to Lex, who kept his weapon fixed on where the android stood.

"We were just on our way out, Mia," Kat said.

In under a second, Mia had disappeared from the landing and moved in a flash to stand directly in front of the group. Kat swallowed her fear and cast her flashlight's beam on the android, who was staring back at her with a wicked grin.

In all their planning, none of Blue Team's members had expected she would actually show her face. Their plans where she was concerned were never successful.

They couldn't afford to hesitate any longer.

"Now!" shrieked Kat.

The sharp blasts of rapid gunfire filled the room. Mia made a series of quick movements to deflect the plasma, sending it ricocheting into the walls, where it hissed and singed holes through the wood. She lunged for Lex, who leapt to the side a moment too late. He was knocked to the ground, and another shot fired from his gun, making contact with the dormant chandelier and sending it to the floor with a crash.

Casey drew her knives at the same instant Kat produced her gun, holding fast to the book with one hand and the weapon with the other. Casey dove toward Mia, slashing at her and attempting to lure her away from Lex. Kat fired at the android's leg. The shot burned into her thigh. Mia fell forward into one of Casey's knives and let out an enraged cry.

As synthetic blood spilled onto the floor, Mia wrenched Casey by the arm toward Kat, slamming one into the other. Kat let out a sharp breath as the impact of Casey's body against hers knocked her across the foyer into the wall and pain splintered through her back at the contact.

"Screw the plan," she said, pushing the words from her aching lungs. Each breath stung, and each movement sent a fresh wave of agony through her chest as she steadied herself on her feet and helped Casey to stand. She was certain one of her ribs was broken. "Move out."

Lex scooped Charlie from the floor, and Casey hurried to their side, forming a barrier between Charlie and Mia, who let out a low laugh.

"You can go, this time. I want you to tell Hartley and the rest of your people that I'm coming. For all of you. There's nowhere you can run that I won't find you."

"Move!" Kat repeated.

Lex shot the security panel, and the door unlatched. The panel's light began to flash a brilliant red. Kat knew the police would be on their way, now, if they hadn't already been alerted by neighbors alarmed by the sounds of gunfire.

The group filtered out onto the lawn, Lex carrying Charlie as Casey moved to Kat's side and helped to support her. Kat's chest was on fire, and she supposed she'd lost what little focus she'd been able to keep on making her walk seem normal. The four made their way down the street toward the black car parked a few houses down along the curb.

"I'm sorry, I'm sorry," Charlie mumbled drowsily.

"Not your fault," said Kat. "Keep moving."

"Derek?" Lila asked the darkness.

She lay on the sofa in Clarisse's living room, her eyes open and strained against the night. She had found herself unable to sleep, and her mind reeled with the wealth of new information she had become privy to over the last few hours.

After explaining her role in Mia's creation, Clarisse had made dinner for Lila, Derek, and Ravenna, and then she had decided to allow them to spend the night. They had agreed for the sake of gathering information. Ravenna was somewhere else in the house in a guest bedroom, and Derek had taken the living room's recliner.

Lila felt that he had kept her in the dark. Why hadn't he mentioned Eddie's military proposal? Was she not an integral part of the company, and had she not deserved to know? She tried to convince herself that Derek had simply never thought about the idea again after Eddie had suggested it, at least until Clarisse's email had surfaced. Nevertheless, doubt had crept into her mind. Was she truly trusted?

"Lila?" Derek sounded half-asleep, and she immediately regretted addressing him, at least until morning.

"How...?" She trailed off with a frown. She wondered how best to broach the subject that she knew was incredibly difficult for him to discuss. Since the accident had occurred, Lila had done her best to refrain from mentioning it. "How did you know what Clarisse was going to say, earlier? About your parents?"

She heard him sigh.

"I don't know. I guess some part of me always knew there was something wrong with the story I was told about it. Someone ran out in front of a van, and the driver swerved to avoid hitting her. He hit my parents' car, and..." He paused. "The driver gave a description of the woman he was trying not to run into, but no one ever found her. That shouldn't have been possible. My dad was a senator—they launched a full investigation and everything. And Eddie seemed to change completely after it happened. I guess it was guilt. I should've known. I should've done something."

"It's not your fault," Lila asserted. "Even if you had figured it out then, what would you have done?"

"I don't know. I really don't."

There was a loud knock at the front door.

Lila jumped. She heard movement in the room and then felt Derek standing beside the sofa. She sat up and glanced down the hall, wondering whether their hostess had heard.

"Clarisse?"

The voice from outside was female, and it sounded desperate.

"Clarisse, it's Blue Team! Let us in!"

Hurried footsteps drew near, and the living room was bathed in light. Lila squinted. Her vision adjusted quickly, and she saw that Clarisse had entered the room and was headed toward the front door. Behind her, Ravenna made her way down the hall at a much slower pace, one hand rubbing her eyes and the other resting on her stomach. She looked quite pale.

Clarisse unlocked the door and opened it. She stepped out of the way, allowing a small group of people to rush in, and then locked the door behind them again.

A woman with red hair stood at the front, looking out of breath and supporting another woman with a wasp tattooed on the side of her neck. Behind them stood a bearded man carrying an unconscious woman with a white-blond ponytail.

"We didn't know where else to go," said the redhead.

Clarisse's expression could've belonged to someone who had just seen a ghost.

"No, it's fine," she said faintly. "What happened? What's wrong with Charlie?" She indicated the unconscious woman. "Set her down, Lex. Over here."

Clarisse waved them over to the sofa. Lila leapt to her feet to give them room, and the man called Lex placed Charlie where Lila had been a moment earlier.

"We thought we could handle it," said the tattooed woman in an undertone. "We were so stupid."

"Handle what, Casey?" Clarisse looked desperate, now.

Utterly confused, Lila moved closer to Derek. He slid an arm around her and watched the newcomers warily.

"Our mission," said Casey. "Our target. Mia."

Lila tensed as Casey knelt beside Charlie and took her pulse at her neck.

"Are you Division?"

All conscious eyes fell on Ravenna, who stood at the edge of the room. She did not falter under their gaze, though she still didn't look entirely well. The redhead frowned and looked from Ravenna to Clarisse and back. Clarisse sighed heavily.

"I didn't have a choice," she said. "They already knew about Mia. They needed to know the rest of the story."

The redhead took a deep breath. "Rachel won't like this."

Clarisse laughed shortly. "Your cousin has more important matters to deal with, by the look of the four of you."

"She's out, Kat," said Casey. "That's not good." She lowered her voice and whispered to Charlie. "You're not allowed to die on me, Blondie." She leaned close and kissed Charlie's cheek.

"Try to wake her up, if you can," said Kat. "She may have hit her head."

"Mia threw her down a flight of stairs," Lex explained as Casey shook Charlie's shoulder. "We went to Dodson's house to look for anything that might connect him to us, and we hoped we'd run into the android. We got our wish."

"Why would you want to see her?" Lila asked, unable to keep herself quiet any longer.

Kat and Clarisse exchanged a glance, and Kat sighed.

"I guess it won't hurt to tell you, considering how much you already know. We're the team that's supposed to be taking her down, and she's outmaneuvered us at every turn."

"Don't take it personally," said Lila with a shake of her head. "She's good at that."

"It seems we have a lot to talk about," said Kat. "And, Clarisse, there's something you should know. She said she's coming for us. All of us. You're in danger."

Silence hung thick in the air for several moments, and then Clarisse sighed.

"What do you want me to do?"

"We're on our way to West Point," said Kat. "I think you should come with us." She paused and looked from Lila and Derek to Ravenna and back to Clarisse. "All of you."

Lila met Derek's eyes and then Ravenna's, and after each of them had nodded, she followed suit. She knew their greatest chance of safety came with staying together, and if that meant merging their small group with this set of Division agents, it improved their odds exponentially.

"I resigned," said Clarisse. "I'm not part of the Division anymore."

"But you were when all of this started," said Lex. "You commissioned her. I'm sorry, but she has more reason to harm you than any of us. That's why you need to come."

Clarisse smiled bitterly. "And you really think you can protect me, if she wants me dead?"

"Go with them," said Ravenna. When Clarisse turned to her with a raised brow, she continued. "Don't be ridiculous. If she's after you, it's the only option."

"Fine," said Clarisse after a beat. "Let's go."

Kat inclined her head appreciatively to Ravenna. "We'll have to take two cars."

"Mine's outside," offered Derek.

"All right. Let's move quickly."

Lex lifted Charlie from the sofa, and everyone filed out onto the lawn, Clarisse shutting the door behind her when she exited. As they walked, Lila watched Kat glance over her shoulder several times on the way to where the agents' black car was parked behind Derek's.

"Not how I expected tonight would go," Ravenna mumbled from Lila's left.

"At least we're getting answers," Lila replied.

Ravenna let out a flat laugh. "The farther we get," she said, "the more I regret asking the questions in the first place."

Chapter Six

Kat scanned her keycard, and the red light over the heavy metal door flicked to green.

"Welcome, Agent Seward," said a computerized voice.

"Everyone come on," instructed Kat.

She and Lex supported a semi-conscious Charlie between them, and Casey limped along behind the trio. Clarisse, Derek, Lila, and Ravenna lingered at the back of the group. Kat knew Clarisse wasn't likely to feel comfortable here anytime soon, and she couldn't entirely blame her. More often than not, Kat envied that Clarisse had had the opportunity to sever her ties with the Division.

As she guided the group through the halls of West Point, they passed military officers who watched them with confusion and the occasional look of unconcealed fear.

"Are you guys okay?" asked a man in dark green fatigues and a patch that read "Captain Herron."

"We're fine," said Kat shortly. "Don't worry about us, Ron."

He nodded slowly and kept walking.

"Lex?"

At the sound of the voice, Lex froze, and Kat did the same. She searched out the speaker, and when her gaze landed on Lex's sister, who was moving toward them at a rapid clip, the corner of her mouth twitched.

"Here it comes," Lex muttered.

"What did she do, put you through a blender?" Abigail demanded as she reached the team.

"I'm fine," Lex said evenly. "Really."

"I don't believe you."

"Abby, I'm fine. Where's Rachel? We need to talk to her."

Abigail's eyes narrowed. "You're worried."

"Where is she?"

Abigail sighed. "Follow me." She turned and started down the hall without another word. Kat exchanged a glance with Lex, who gave a half-shrug.

"She worries too much," he muttered.

"It's because she loves you," said Kat.

"I know."

The group followed Abigail through the building's winding grey halls, and she led them to a closed door with an engraved nameplate at its center. It read "HARTLEY, R." Beneath the name were the words "Division President."

"She's not in a good mood," Abigail warned.

Lex nodded. "We'll deal with that. Thank you." He gave her shoulder a small squeeze.

Abigail opened her mouth as though to speak, but she appeared to think better of whatever she'd been planning to say. Instead, she turned away and started off down the hall again.

Kat surveyed those remaining. Charlie still hovered somewhere between consciousness and oblivion, and Casey was wearing a neutral expression that was a bit too carefully controlled. Kat could see the anger behind it. She knew Casey well enough to know she blamed herself for letting Mia escape and for Charlie's current state. Casey met Kat's eyes briefly, and Kat gave her an attempt at a smile she meant to be comforting. Casey looked away, apparently unwilling to acknowledge the gesture.

Derek, Lila, and Ravenna stood together at the back of the group behind a visibly unhappy Clarisse.

Oh, Rachel's going to love this.

Taking a deep breath, Kat knocked on the door.

"Who is it?" called Rachel's voice from the other side.

"Blue Team," said Kat.

"Come in."

Kat pulled open the door. Shelves full of books and files dominated the left wall, and a desk sat facing the door at the back of the room.

Rachel was perched on the edge of the desk, ankles crossed, her false smile doing its best to hide the distress in her eyes. Leaning against the wall opposite the door was Andrew, who looked as though he'd just been about to speak but had paused upon Kat's appearance.

Rachel slid off the desk and approached the door, looking from Kat to Charlie, and her expression lost its pretense and shifted to visible panic.

"Is she conscious?" she asked Kat.

"Barely. She's nodded off a few times, and she needs medical attention."

"Lex, Casey, take her to the infirmary, please," said Rachel.

Kat shifted her portion of Charlie's weight to Casey, whose lips twisted downward. Kat knew Casey had been trying to avoid losing her self-control by processing just how injured her girlfriend was, and her stomach twisted at the blend of guilt and pain in Casey's expression.

Kat leaned close to speak into Casey's ear.

"This is not your fault. At all. And she's going to be okay."

Casey nodded stiffly. "Thanks," she mumbled.

"Get yourself looked at, too," Kat added.

"Will do."

Casey and Lex escorted Charlie from the room, and then Kat turned back to Rachel.

"It was stupid of us to even try to ambush Mia," she said. "She's always ten steps ahead."

"I'm a little more worried about why it took you so long to get back here," said Rachel with a shake of her head. "With Charlie like that, it's irresponsible."

Kat squared her shoulders. "I made an executive decision, and I'm sorry it delayed us so long."

Rachel arched a brow. "What decision was that?"

"Mia gave us a message for you. She said she's coming for all of us. And since we were within about an hour's drive of Clarisse, we went ahead and picked her up."

Rachel's expression softened slightly. "All right. Are you hurt?"

Kat hesitated. Her back ached from its impact with the wall in Dodson's foyer, and she wondered if her broken rib had damaged any internal organs.

"Get yourself to the infirmary and get checked out,"

Rachel pressed on, evidently taking Kat's silence as an affirmative answer. "Afterward, I need you to get word to McNaire as soon as humanly possible. Tell him we don't know how wide of a net Mia's casting but that he needs to lie low until we do. I'm going to run over our security protocols here and recall everyone I can reach."

"Do you think bringing them all here is safe?" asked Kat. "She knows where we are; she was tested here. West Point doesn't seem like the best option."

"I don't know," Rachel admitted with a sigh. "I'd like to think our defenses can keep her out, and the others, if…" She trailed off, frowning, and glanced at Andrew, who still stood stoically beside the back wall. His lips were pressed into a thin line.

Kat knew exactly what the others were thinking. No one wanted to acknowledge how awful things could get if Mia was working with Osiris and his band of rogue androids.

"I'll give them the option," Rachel said at last. "If they want to stick it out here and help us fight if it comes to that, good. If they'd rather risk it out there, fine. But I want them to be informed."

"Roger," said Kat with a nod. She turned for the door and paused at the sight of the civilians standing in the hallway and looking severely uncomfortable. "Rachel, there are a few people here we owe an explanation."

Without another word, Kat limped out of the office.

Rachel folded her arms, suppressing the urge to sigh. She knew her cousin was stubborn, but Kat's resistance to admitting when she needed medical treatment grated on Rachel, who had promised both her mother and her Aunt Elena that she would keep Kat safe to the best of her ability. Dangerous missions were inevitable, but seeking help for injuries was an option Kat often disregarded while trying to be strong enough for everyone.

Mia's threat still hung at the front of Rachel's mind.

Does this mean Mom's in danger? Considering she's not involved with the Division anymore, I'd like to hope she's safe, but… I need to make sure.

"Rachel."

Her focus returned to the present as Clarisse Mitchell stepped into the room, pain evident in her eyes. It had been years since the two women had last spoken. After Mia had caused yet another accident, this time only blocks from West Point, Clarisse had had enough. She had resigned, and control of the Division had passed to the then-twenty-four-year-old Rachel. Despite Rachel's attempts—and those of her organization at large—to contact Clarisse for information over the past six years, Clarisse had wanted absolutely nothing to do with them.

"Clarisse." Rachel inclined her head to the elder woman. "I didn't expect you to come back. But I'm glad you did," she added swiftly.

Clarisse gave a short laugh. The sound was clipped, somewhat scornful.

"I didn't plan on it," she said. "I promised myself I would never set foot in this place again."

Rachel swallowed. She heard Andrew start toward her from the room's rear, but she kept her attention on Clarisse.

"What changed your mind?" she asked quietly.

"Your cousin. She insisted. She thinks Mia's going to try to kill me."

Silence filled the office, thick and oppressive.

"If what happened to Blue Team is any indication," Andrew began, stopping at Rachel's side, "she can do much more than try. If they hadn't left when they did, I doubt they would still be alive."

Clarisse studied him for a moment and then sighed. "I know them. I've watched them train since Lex transferred from the Air Force almost eight years ago. I know what they're capable of. The fact that they weren't able to take her down scared the hell out of me. That's why I'm here. Mia can do what she wants to me. This whole mess is my fault, anyway."

"Clarisse," said Rachel, alarmed, "you couldn't have known she would—"

"That's not the point. It's my fault, and I'm here to make sure it gets taken care of. For good, this time."

Clarisse looked over her shoulder, and Rachel followed her gaze to a man whose presence she hadn't yet noticed as three people followed Clarisse into the room. At the sight of him, her mouth went dry.

Derek Lawrence. One of the heads of Lawrence-Dodson Enterprises, former business partner of Mia's creator, and son of two of her victims.

Rachel's stomach twisted. These things weren't her fault, but she felt no less responsible for them than Clarisse or than her own mother, who had commissioned Mia. After a failed attempt on her life many years earlier, Isabella was no longer in a state to deal with problems like these, and after Clarisse's abdication, Rachel had felt she'd been the only one left who could tie up the loose ends the Division had left. Now, her time was running out. In addition to Mia's threats, she had those of the president to handle. If Mia wasn't found soon, the Division would be all but disbanded by the time McNaire realized exactly how much he needed it.

Rachel pushed these thoughts away and did her best to focus on Derek.

"Mr. Lawrence," she greeted him. "It's an honor to finally meet you."

Derek blinked. "Thank you," he said, "but the honor is mine. I saw you on the telesense with your mother all the time when I was growing up. I think my sister idolized you."

Rachel laughed. His words had reminded her of a much happier time, when she had been just a child following around her famous mother, blissfully unaware of the secrets the adult world hid from her.

"Well, thank you," she said. Her eyes flicked to the blond woman at his side. She was beautiful, not a single imperfection visible to Rachel's eye, and her smile was radiant as the two women exchanged glances. "And Lila?" Rachel asked, more out of politeness than inquiry, as she knew the woman could be no one else.

Lila nodded. "It's great to meet you, Miss Hartley."

"Likewise." Rachel moved closer to them, shaking each of their hands in turn. Her acknowledgement was earnest. For years, the Division had attempted to reach the level of flawlessness Lila exemplified in an android, and for years, that goal had eluded them like a prize just out of arms' reach. "I've heard so much about you."

"Wait a second, Andrew?"

At Derek's words, Andrew let out a small laugh.

"I'm sorry, Mr. Lawrence. I didn't expect to be recalled quite so soon. When we figured out that you knew about the Division, we saw no point in me keeping my cover."

"You… were a plant? Were you spying on us?"

"No, no, not at all," Andrew assured him. "I was trying to locate Mia and help Blue Team capture her. I'm sorry I couldn't stop her before she did more damage."

Derek let out a long breath, and he seemed to deflate. "I appreciate you trying," he said.

Rachel looked from Derek to the last figure, and her heart jumped into her throat. The woman had Clarisse's eyes, and her hair was nearly black. Rachel remembered this face, though she hadn't seen the other woman in more than a decade.

"Ravenna?"

The woman in question nodded, though the tight smile she gave was clearly uncomfortable.

"I didn't think you remembered me," she said.

"Of course I do." An image of two teenagers chatting animatedly at the back of Air Force One flashed through Rachel's mind, followed by several of the same two girls wearing pajamas and building pillow forts at the White House. These were followed by something thoroughly different, which led Rachel's smile to falter.

She sat at the back of her mother's limousine, working hard to pretend she wasn't listening to the conversation beyond the partition separating her from her mother and Clarisse. Rachel doubted whether she should really be here. She was on a break from her third semester at Juilliard and had accompanied Isabella to West Point at the elder woman's request. It seemed that Isabella hoped her daughter would one day take more of an interest in what was happening behind the governmental curtain than she currently did. Truth be told, while the Division's dealings did interest Rachel to an extent—now that she'd been made aware of its existence, several years after its creation—she wanted no part in politics. What she had seen her mother go through over the years to reach her current position was more than enough for one lifetime.

Rachel didn't know whether her mother would give her the full story as to what she was discussing with Clarisse after they had returned to Washington, and she couldn't deny that she was curious what had been important enough to warrant this meeting.

"She's done it," said Clarisse's voice from the other side of the partition.

"He's been neutralized?" asked Isabella.

"Yes. And what you promised? Ravenna will be cleared of all charges?"

"I wouldn't lie to you, Clarisse. Her record will be destroyed, after I see him for myself."

The memory was unwelcome, and Rachel banished it. Ravenna was here, standing in front of her, and unharmed, as far as one could tell. That would be enough to keep Rachel from fretting over the past that she had been unable to stop, at least for now.

"You two know each other?"

Andrew's voice drew her more firmly into the present. He looked from her to the newcomers and back.

"Yes," said Rachel. "Ravenna is Clarisse's niece. We spent quite a bit of time together when my mother was in office."

Andrew smiled and offered his hand to Ravenna, who shook it somewhat hesitantly.

Rachel glanced at the holographic readout of the time projected on the wall to her left, and she inhaled sharply. 1:56. *When did that happen?*

"I'd love to talk with each of you more, but I think it'll have to wait until you've had some rest. It's almost two in the morning, and I'm sure you're all exhausted."

Ravenna nodded quickly. Whether she was eager to escape the situation at hand or simply agreeing, Rachel didn't know.

"Forgive us," said Derek. "It's been a very long day, and we've learned a lot all at once."

He looked to Andrew, enough surprise evident in his expression to suggest that he still couldn't believe his employee had been a Division agent.

"We understand," said Andrew. "We'll have to figure out later just how much 'a lot' is." He smirked. "National security and all that."

Ravenna let out a humorless laugh. "Naturally."

Rachel looked past them into the hallway, calling out to the nearest officer.

"Bates."

The freckled, camouflage-suited man hustled forward to stand behind the group.

"Yes, ma'am?"

"Would you please show our friends to the guest quarters?"

"Certainly, ma'am," said Bates. "Follow me, please."

He turned and led the way down the corridor. Derek nodded to Rachel and Andrew and moved after him along with Lila. Ravenna left a few seconds later, her expression unreadable as she turned away. Clarisse lingered.

"I hope you've got some kind of plan," she told Rachel. "A better one than I had."

Rachel smiled sadly. "Unfortunately, it seems our plans have changed. Goodnight, Clarisse."

Without another word, Clarisse followed the others.

"You should get some rest, too," said Andrew. Rachel turned to find him watching her with unconcealed concern.

"I will," she said. "Eventually."

"You can't go on like this, Rachel. It's not healthy. If there's the slightest bit of work to be done, you don't sleep, you don't eat. When are you going to understand that the rest of us are here to help you so that you don't need to live like this?"

She laid her hands on his shoulders and looked into his brown eyes. His cologne smelled vaguely of cinnamon.

"I know that, Andrew," she said. "I'm just worried. That's all."

He pulled her close, and she gave in to the comfort she felt in his arms and rested her head against his chest.

"We'll take care of it," he said. "I won't let Mia hurt you."

She wanted to argue that if a highly trained Division special-operations team couldn't defeat Mia, Andrew on his own didn't stand much of a chance. Instead, she let herself be soothed by the idea that she knew he would try, if only for her.

"I know," she said.

"I love you," said Andrew.

"I love you, too."

Chapter Seven

The steady thump of the bassline through the speakers sent pain crackling through Desi's head with each beat. She mentally cursed herself for allowing Marley and Lucy to drag her out, and she wanted nothing more than to be home beneath several layers of blankets with her door locked and barricaded.

Each time someone bumped into her on the dancefloor, her heart leapt into her throat. With each accidental brush of a shoulder or hand against her arm, she was certain the limb belonged to Eddie or to Mia and that she would be dragged out of the bar and to some unimaginable torture.

Maybe Ben was right, she thought bitterly as she drained another shot of tequila. *Maybe I should see someone.*

She fumbled through her purse until she found her phone. Her lock screen was blank apart from her wallpaper, which was a photo of herself standing with Damian that she'd taken at his birthday party back in June.

Derek still hadn't called.

Desi looked around to find Lucy dancing unsteadily, her red ponytail swinging in time with her hips. Marley leaned against the wall nearby, talking to a woman Desi didn't recognize, and Desi approached the pair, and laid a hand on her friend's arm.

"Keep an eye on her," she said, despising how loudly she had to speak to ensure that Marley could hear her over the music. She didn't particularly want to leave either of them unattended, but she had to check on her brother.

She wouldn't forgive herself if she made the same mistake twice.

"Where are you going?" Marley called back to her.

"Phone."

Desi held up the device and then started across the room, weaving through the writhing mass of bodies on her way out the side door. When she reached the alley, she let out a breath she hadn't realized she'd been holding.

She had always enjoyed nights like this. Since childhood, she'd loved to dance, and the alcohol sometimes helped her to forget that she wouldn't go home to her parents or her eldest brother or the man she—

Stop it, she ordered herself. She rubbed at her temple and leaned her head back against the wall.

Tonight, she'd been drinking to forget Eddie. Naturally it hadn't worked even a bit, but she had at least found an excuse to leave her apartment and had finally gotten her friends to stop bothering her about becoming a recluse.

Still, coming out with Marley and Lucy had only confirmed what she'd already believed. This life had lost its appeal to her.

She pressed her finger to her phone's surface and mentally ordered it to call Derek. He picked up on the first ring.

"Is something wrong?"

Desi sighed. "Nice to hear from you, too."

"I only ask because it's after two," said Derek. "I didn't call because I hoped at least one of us was getting to sleep."

"Not likely."

"What's that noise?"

Desi glanced toward the door she'd exited through and the source of the persistent pounding bass.

"Marley and Lucy dragged me out," she muttered. "I don't want to be here." Before Derek could comment, Desi pressed onward. "Where are you? I thought you were coming back after you found Clarisse."

"We were going to, but…" Derek paused. "I don't know how much I'm allowed to tell you. It's complicated."

"I'd say I have a right to know, at this point." Desi regretted snapping as soon as she'd spoken, but her splitting headache and exhaustion were making it difficult to keep herself calm.

"It's not that. The Division found us, and they brought us with Clarisse to their base. I don't have a lot of information yet, but as soon as I do, you'll be the first to know."

"What is the Division?" Desi pressed.

"They were created to design android soldiers," Derek explained. "Their first wave went extremely wrong, and a lot of people died. They asked Eddie to make Mia as a second attempt."

Desi frowned. What had given Eddie the right to use LDE's research for his own ends? To weaponize it?

"And you didn't know about any of this?" she asked.

"No. Well, he asked Damian and me once if we would consider something like that, but we told him no. We had no idea he actually went through with it. I can't say anything else yet, but I swear I'll tell you as soon as I can."

Desi glanced down the alley and caught sight of a shadow at its end.

"Okay," she said quickly. "Keep me updated, and stay safe. That's an order."

"I will," said Derek. "Promise."

As soon as the line went dead, Desi slipped back into the bar, determined to locate her friends and remain with them until she was safe within her apartment.

Ravenna lay awake in the darkness long after Lila's breathing had settled into a rhythmic, automatic pattern in the bunk above her. Derek was in a room down the hall, and since Lila was asleep, Ravenna felt incredibly alone in this strange place that she had visited only once before with her aunt.

She doubted she would ever feel safe enough here to sleep. Who was to say that someone wouldn't burst in the second she let her guard down, having finally realized the actions that were tied to her name, and arrest her?

There was something off about Rachel when she recognized me, she thought. *I bet she knows. She knows what I've done, and she's debating what to do with me.*

Ravenna wondered if their adolescent friendship would be enough to save her, if it came down to it. She knew Rachel had power. If the former First Daughter and current Division President wanted to allow Ravenna to walk free, it was probably possible. But would Rachel want that, if she knew how many people Ravenna had killed?

Sighing into the blackness around her, Ravenna asked herself what she would do, if their places were reversed. What if she were in a position of power, with the ability to pardon people of their crimes? What if Rachel had killed people? What if she had then evaded the law for years until one day appearing unannounced at a military training facility that doubled as headquarters for a covert government group?

In truth, Ravenna had no idea what she would do. She doubted Rachel would have ever gotten into this position.

Her target was a serial killer.

That didn't make what she was about to do right, though it did make her feel the smallest bit better about it. Through taking one life, she would be saving many more.

Her client had neglected to tell her his name, but he had promised her a large sum of money, if she succeeded.

Ravenna, age eighteen, sat cross-legged on the roof of an old apartment building, her dark clothing cloaking her in the night. She strained her eyes for any indication of movement from the parking lot below and ignored the pulse pounding in her ears.

Keep it together, Rae. Now isn't the time to lose it.

It was unseasonably cool for September, and Ravenna wished she had thought to wear something warmer than the thin, long-sleeved black shirt and slacks that she had chosen. She absentmindedly fiddled with the gold bracelet on her right wrist, which, if caught in the right light, could give away her position and ruin her plan. She couldn't find it within herself to care. It rarely ever left her arm. The golden accessory had been a gift from Aunt Clarisse, and each time Ravenna recalled her aunt's bravery in her work for President Hartley, she felt stronger.

She let out a sigh at the thought of what her aunt would say about her present course of action.

The sound carried farther than she had anticipated, and she bit her lip, chastising herself for her lack of focus.

Suddenly, she saw him.

Across the parking lot in front of the apartment building, a man wearing clothing similar to her own had exited a silver hovercar. He strode purposefully across the lot, hands shoved into his pockets and head lowered, probably to avoid attracting attention.

Ravenna took a deep breath and let it out silently, releasing the golden chain links at her wrist and picking up the weapon that lay beside her.

She had practiced shooting the plasma gun many times under Roman's tutelage, but never at a human. This was her first attempt at holding her own with a target.

He strode beneath a lamp, and his face was illuminated. All doubts that she had possessed as to whether this was the right person were erased. His chin was covered by a dark, scruffy beard, and a glint of gold at his earlobe caught the light. The photo she had received from her client had been, undeniably, of this man.

Her heart pounded as she trained the weapon on him, adjusting its position as he walked toward the building. If she didn't act quickly, she knew her chance would evaporate.

Fighting to keep her hands steady and her breathing under control, she steeled herself to what she had to do. There was no turning back.

Ravenna fired.

The shot made contact with her target's lower leg, causing him to lose his balance and crumple to the asphalt beneath him. He cried out, pushing himself up onto his hands to search the area for his assailant.

Surely someone had heard the shot. Ravenna had to make this quick if she was going to be gone before anyone came looking for the source of the noise.

She took aim once again.

In one terrible instant, her resolve was shaken. Her target looked up, and she was certain that he had seen her. He looked directly at the spot in which she had felt completely concealed. She panicked.

Her hands instinctively tightened around the weapon, and she squeezed the trigger.

The second shot was a direct hit to the chest. Her target fell backward, unmoving.

Without hesitation, Ravenna stood, running to the edge of the building and leaping onto the rickety landing of the fire escape. She slid down the ladder and landed on her feet with a thump on the ground below.

She gulped.

Oh, shit. I parked on the other side of…

Voices were approaching. She had to leave. Now.

As fast as her legs would carry her, she ran across the sparsely lit parking lot. The thudding of her heart mingled with the thudding of her boots against the pavement as she fled toward her car, which was parked just three spots from her target's.

She skidded to a halt only feet away from the man she had just shot. Gingerly, she inched closer, casting her eyes downward.

The man spluttered and spat up blood onto his cheek.
"Are—are you—an angel?" he asked faintly.
Tears stung her eyes, and she ran.
Maybe the angel of death, *she thought.*

The group moved swiftly through the base, their feet falling in a rapid succession of dull thuds. Clarisse's heart pounded in her ears as she moved along with Isabella at the group's center, flanked by Secret Service personnel. This was it. Though she remained to the public the president's secretary, most of her waking hours were spent supervising the Division's progress from afar. She had to keep up appearances, for the time being. The nation could not yet be privy to what was happening behind the closed doors of West Point. Clarisse could not afford to be seen here, not yet. She couldn't be connected to the project until a certain amount of progress had been made, and it appeared that, today, that time was upon her.

Her mind drifted for a moment to her niece, who was waiting with the president's daughter in a room on the opposite side of the building, oblivious to why they were all here. Clarisse wished she could explain to Ravenna what was going on, but at this point, she herself wasn't quite sure.

They had finished. That was all she knew. But this was only part of the overall goal. Would the final product work?

Clarisse and Isabella were ushered into a dimly lit hallway and into a small, cramped room that Clarisse didn't think would accommodate them all. Isabella must have decided the same thing, as she instructed the Secret Service agents to wait outside the door and allow Clarisse and herself to remain.

Though they protested, she insisted and shut the door after they had gone.

The opposite wall was dominated by a large mirror, which Isabella approached. Clarisse assumed that the president knew what she was doing, and she followed her lead.

"Welcome, Madam President and Ms. Mitchell."

Clarisse jumped. She looked around for the source of the voice and located a speaker hanging from the ceiling in the corner.

"Thank you for coming."

"What have you got for us?" asked Isabella.

"A group of prototype androids has been completed."

As the voice spoke, the mirror changed. Lights ignited on the other side, turning it into a window. Clarisse blinked, taking in the transformation.

On the other side of the glass was an enormous, sunken room, the floor of which had to be at least twenty feet below where Clarisse and Isabella stood. Military personnel lined the walls, clutching weapons in a way that looked more defensive than offensive. At the center of the room, seven figures stood in a line, staring directly in front of them.

As Clarisse watched, the one in the center looked up into the glass. He was dark-haired and olive-skinned, his jaw set tightly.

"Can they see us?" Clarisse whispered.

"Not in the way we consider 'seeing,' no," said the voice on the speaker. Clarisse fought the urge to react. She hadn't anticipated the voice would hear her; her question had been directed more toward Isabella. "However," the voice continued, "they are designed to detect heat. So, in a manner of speaking, yes. Though they don't know who you are."

The thought was vaguely unsettling to Clarisse. She said no more.

The sound of a mug being set down on the desk drew Clarisse from her memories and back into Rachel's office. She looked up to find Abigail Knight standing before her. Abigail nodded to the cup, concern visible in her eyes.

"It might wake you up."

Clarisse nodded and smiled. "Thank you." She grasped the mug with both hands, allowing its warmth to fill her. Bringing it to her nose, she inhaled, taking in the scent of coffee and French vanilla creamer.

I need this, she thought. *It's not like I slept last night.*

She had tossed and turned well into the morning, unable to find peace enough to rest now that she had come back to the place where the most haunting moments of her life had occurred. Painful recollections tormented her with every passing moment. She wondered bitterly if being found by Mia would be less tortuous than reliving this phase of her past.

"Thanks," she told Abigail again.

The girl nodded, taking a seat beside Clarisse. On the opposite side of the desk, in the place Clarisse herself had once occupied, sat her successor. Dark, heavy crescents lined the bottoms of Rachel's eyelids, and Clarisse wondered if the younger woman's night had been as difficult as her own. With ill-concealed hesitation, Rachel directed her attention to Clarisse.

"I trust you remember the Seven."

Clarisse choked on her coffee. "How could I forget?" She asked, frowning deeply.

Rachel ignored the question. "We've been monitoring the targets since our attempt failed. Thus far, we've learned that they all follow a similar pattern. They blend in to human society to avoid being detected, and if they realize one of our people is onto them, they immediately relocate."

"If you know all this," said Clarisse as her frown deepened, "why haven't you made another attempt?"

Rachel opened her mouth, but Abigail spoke hurriedly.

"They haven't harmed anyone. They've appeared to simply want to live in peace, to be left alone. We didn't feel it was necessary to act without cause. But now..."

"Now?" prompted Clarisse.

"Now they've disappeared." Rachel sighed heavily. "Fallen completely off the map. We're blind."

Clarisse felt the mug begin to slip from her hands, and she placed it on the desk before she could cause any more destruction. "What?"

"We lost them." Rachel closed her eyes and folded her hands on her desk, seemingly preparing herself for the reprimand that Clarisse was too shocked to give.

"What the hell does this mean?"

"We think they're planning something," said Abigail. "What that could be, we don't know. But I'm sure they remember that we took one of them out the last time they made a move, and I doubt they've forgotten it."

A thought occurred to Clarisse, troubling beyond measure and too plausible for comfort. The disappearance of the targets the Division had been monitoring coincided too perfectly with the threat made by another android.

"You don't think...?" she breathed, unable to finish the question.

"That they're in league with Mia?" inquired Rachel bluntly. "We don't know. As I said, we're blind, now. We have no way of knowing what they're planning to do or who they're working with. But I know that I feel less safe here with every day that passes. I've spent the night poring over our defenses, and we aren't equipped for this. I don't intend to endanger the lives of countless people by continuing to work from West Point if we think there's even the slightest possibility that a group of homicidal androids may have us in their sights."

Despite how grave their situation could prove to be, Clarisse found herself deeply impressed. When she'd left the Division, it had been without a clue or expectation as to who would replace her. She had done her best to avoid thinking about the organization over the intervening years. However, she now realized that the leader chosen after her possessed the same conviction and capability as herself.

Bravo, Rachel. I can only hope that it doesn't cost you as much as it cost me.

Chapter Eight

Desi vaguely processed the room around her—the soft sheets enveloping her, the cushion of the pillow beneath her head. No light attempted to filter through her eyelids, and she felt the warmth of an arm around her waist.

She breathed in and out again, reveling in the comfortable silence.

Then she froze.

Why was there an arm around her?

She opened her eyes and turned over so quickly the room around her blurred.

She stifled the scream that sought to burst from her throat the sight of Eddie lying beside her. Still, he stirred and blinked awake, watching her with a raised brow.

"What's the matter?" he asked.

He lifted a hand to rub his eyes, and his fingers were covered in blood.

She sat up with a shriek, scanning her bedroom to find that it was after sunrise and that there was no one else in sight.

Slowly, she crossed her legs and lowered her face into her hands. Several moments passed in silence apart from her deep breaths.

He's not here. He's never going to be here again.

Desi climbed out of bed and pulled on the robe she'd draped over the chair at her dresser, and she made her way into the living room.

In the doorway, she came to a halt. She gasped, her hands flying to her mouth.

The sofa and chairs had been overturned, as had the coffee table. The telesense screen was cracked down the middle.

Desi crept forward, and in the kitchen doorway, she saw shards of glass and porcelain from what she knew had to be broken china.

"Hello?"

Her voice trembled, but she did not falter. She scanned the apartment, searching the kitchen, the living room, the bedroom, and the bathroom before she eventually sank onto the sofa. Her breathing was shallow and her pulse was rapid, but she knew she was alone.

She grabbed her phone from the end table and willed it to call Marley.

Derek hesitated at the door, his fist raised to knock.

He hadn't spoken with Lila since they had been shown to separate accommodations in the early hours of the morning. Since the discovery of the degree of Eddie's deception and of Derek's one-time knowledge of the idea of Mia's creation—though not that Eddie had actually gone through with it—Lila had appeared distant. It seemed her faith in Derek had been shaken by the revelations of the last twenty-four hours, and he couldn't stand it. They had only just begun repairing the damage Eddie and Mia had caused, and he couldn't stand the thought that the progress they had made could be undone. It wasn't as though he had intended to keep her or anyone else in the dark; Eddie had done enough of that to last a lifetime. Derek had, in truth, never considered the possibility that his former business partner could have done such things without the knowledge of either Lawrence brother.

But before the group had reached West Point, Lila had taken his hand twice, and she hadn't rejected him when his reflex had been to wrap an arm around her as the agents had ruined whatever illusion they had still possessed of normalcy. But why? Did she feel something for him, or was she simply looking for someone familiar to cling to as the world fell to pieces?

He needed to see her.

He knocked, and a few moments later, he heard movement from the other side of the door followed by muffled voices.

The door opened, and Ravenna stood on the threshold. Her posture was tense, and she looked prepared to strike at an instant's provocation, but her demeanor shifted as her focus fell on Derek. She relaxed and glanced over her shoulder to where Lila sat on the bottom bunk, watching him. The room was as small and cramped as his own, the only difference that it held enough occupants for both of its bunks.

"I don't imagine you're here to see me," said Ravenna. "I'll be around, if anyone needs anything." She slipped past Derek and started down the hall without another word.

Lila offered him a small smile. "Good morning."

"Morning." Derek stepped into the room and closed the door behind him. Lila patted the thin mattress beside her, and he sat. "How did you sleep?" he asked.

She shrugged. "Fine. What about you?"

"Not well. There's something about being here that's just... off, to me."

"I can understand that."

There was silence.

"Lila, I wanted to ask you something."

She gave an almost imperceptible frown. "Sure, what is it?"

"Did what I told you last night change the way you feel about me? When I mentioned that Eddie had spoken to me about a military android?"

Lila closed her eyes. She was lost to her thoughts for what felt like an eternity to him. His heart pounded as he waited for her to speak, and when she finally did, he let out a small, relieved breath.

"Derek, nothing is going to make me think less of you. But I want you to be honest with me. I don't want secrets. Since you restored my memories, I've wanted to feel like things are back to normal between us, or... as normal as they can be, at least. I want to feel like you trust me."

He took her hand, and she opened her eyes to meet his.

"I do trust you," he asserted. "With my life."

She smiled. "That's good to hear."

His stomach twisted slightly at what he'd said. He knew that when Lila was in control of her actions, she would never even consider harming him or anyone else. He squashed down the tiny part of himself that feared she could become compromised again.

He also knew that if he was going to create an atmosphere of trust, he had to offer her something, had to let her see that he had no need for secrets.

"There's something I want to tell you. Please understand why I haven't mentioned it before now; this is a project that I haven't had any part of in years, and the only other people who ever knew about it were Damian and Eddie."

Lila nodded slowly. "Go on."

"You remember how devastated I was after I lost my parents."

"Of course."

"I certainly wasn't the only one. The three of us wanted to do something to honor them. We began considering the prospect of preserving one's memories after their death. Ideas, experiences, things that could be beneficial to those left behind and could keep their loved one around in some form. We'd already become successful creating androids not based on any specific person. We wondered, why couldn't the same principles apply to an android that was? Not only based on someone, but designed to be him? To think like him, act like him, believe he was that person? What if we could find a way to transfer thoughts, feelings, memories, and someone's very essence into an android modeled in his image?"

Lila's pale blue eyes were wide as she listened intently. "Did you succeed?" she asked.

She's not angry, he thought. *She's interested. It's better than I hoped for.*

A knock sounded at the door.

Derek sighed, releasing Lila's hand and crossing the room. He opened the door to find Abigail Knight standing on the other side.

"I hope I'm not interrupting anything." She glanced from Derek to Lila and back again, and she didn't wait for either of them to speak before continuing. "Ms. Hartley's in a meeting right now, but as soon as it ends, she would like to speak with you both."

"Ravenna, wait!"

With a sigh, she halted in her steps down the grey-walled corridor and turned to face her aunt. Clarisse was out of breath; she looked like she had been running.

"I need to talk to you," she said.

"About what, Aunt Clarisse? Something else you've kept from me for years?"

Ravenna no longer cared if her words stung. She had been lied to for too long. Now she was in danger, as were her friends and her unborn child. The longer she stayed here, the angrier she became. Rachel had the power to do whatever she liked to punish her for her crimes, and Ravenna couldn't forgive Clarisse for the years spent defending her honor against accusations that had turned out to be only a tenth of the full truth.

Clarisse glanced up and down the corridor, presumably scanning for people near enough to hear her. After a moment, she said, "We need to go somewhere more private. I have a room, if you'll come with me."

Ravenna rolled her eyes. "Fine."

She followed her aunt to a room much like the one she had been assigned, down to the same grey bedding and empty walls. Clarisse took a seat at the small table in the corner. She folded her hands and rested her chin on them, watching as Ravenna sat opposite her.

"This… is a difficult discussion to have," said Clarisse. "And, technically, I'm not allowed to tell you any of it."

Ravenna quirked an eyebrow. "Let me get this straight. You're going against the Division's orders to tell me something, when you've been going along with whatever they tell you to do for years, despite the fact that it has endangered my life as well as those of people I care about?"

Clarisse sighed, closing her eyes and pressing her fingertips to her temple. "I wish you would stop being so difficult. Don't you understand that if I could have let you in on any of this when you were visiting me in Washington all those years ago, I would have? That in the intervening years, I've wanted nothing more than a chance to make things right with you? That I would give anything to undo some of the horrible things I've done, most of all what I've done to you?"

There was silence. Ravenna had grown good enough at reading people to understand that the pain in her aunt's lined face was genuine.

"Okay. Then tell me."

Taking in a deep breath, Clarisse flattened her hands on the table. "Do you remember a target by the name of Ra?"

Ravenna's fingernails dug into her palms as her fists clenched. She felt the color drain from her face, and her mouth went dry. She forced out only one word.

"Yes."

Clarisse nodded. "Can you tell me everything you remember about when you killed him?"

Ravenna swallowed hard, forcing herself to focus. As she recalled the details, she described them to her aunt.

Everything about this hit felt wrong.

Ravenna had been hired to take out a target in Washington, D.C. Her rational side had screamed at her not to agree, as the odds of being caught were considerably higher here than most any other place she could have gone. But her heart had become hollow, and she had nothing to lose. The only thing of any value to her was on her wrist, tucked beneath the arm of the black sweater she'd chosen to block out the biting wind. She'd received the bracelet before leaving home as soon as she'd graduated high school. It was the twin to Aunt Clarisse's, and the reminder of the relative Ravenna had always admired most was welcome when she hadn't seen anyone in her family for years.

As though the overwhelming presence of the law in the city hadn't been difficult enough to navigate to get to the spot where her mark was supposed to be, the lack of information provided by her employer complicated matters. Ravenna knew nothing about the man she was to kill apart from his name. No history, no justification for what she planned to do.

When choosing her clients over the years, she had elected to gravitate toward the targets who were guilty of one thing or another. It helped her sleep at night to know that some good might come of her actions, if only in the form of the prevention of future wrongs. She viewed herself as an agent of karma.

Now, however, things were different. She had no idea who the man known only as "Ra" really was, only that she was tasked with killing him.

Ravenna leaned against a wall in an alleyway, awaiting her moment of opportunity as she blended into the darkness. Her target was expected to pass this way within the hour, if her information was correct. The shops nearby had all closed for the night, and so far, Ravenna had only seen a few sets of headlights pass.

A group of tourists drifted down the sidewalk in front of the alley, chatting loudly. They looked around the right age to be high school students, and Ravenna's chest clenched at the sight of them.

"Let's hope someone doesn't get herself separated from the group again tomorrow," said one of the passersby, poking her companion in the shoulder.

"It wasn't my fault! I left my phone at the hotel! I wanted to call you, but I couldn't. Besides, the one time I was actually lost, none of you realized it until I showed up again and scared the hell out of you."

"The flight simulator was incredible," said a boy walking behind the first pair.

"It was," said the girl beside him with a nod. "I still can't believe I was actually good at the guns."

Their voices gradually faded, their words mingling with laughter.

They're happy.

Ravenna wished more than anything to return to that age. In just a few short years, she'd lost everything she'd loved about her life, and there were days she couldn't recognize herself in the mirror. She couldn't recall the last time she had been genuinely happy.

After the group's voices had deserted the area, a lone figure passed, his hands in his pockets and his vision directed toward the sidewalk.

Several seconds after he was clear of the alley, Ravenna slipped silently into the street after him. Her feet fell on the pavement in precise time with his, and she had almost convinced herself that things would go according to plan.

"You're not bad at this," said the man.

Ravenna's heart leapt into her throat.

"Not fantastic, but not bad."

The man turned to face her, and his features were caught in the glow of a streetlamp. His skin was olive, and his dark hair was pulled back behind his head. His eyes were a startlingly bright shade of green, and they held a kind of dark fire she had never seen.

She reached for the plasma gun at her side and drew it in a flash. Returning her attention to where her target should have been, she found that he had disappeared. She scowled and opened her mouth, but before she could make a sound, she heard his voice at her ear.

"Right here."

Ravenna jumped, whipping around to face him. She pointed the gun at his heart, and he slid to the side and into the next alley more quickly than she had ever seen anyone move.

"Not fantastic," he said.

The taunts and the fear surging through Ravenna set her on edge. She fought to remain focused. To anticipate.

I can't fire until I get a shot. The second I do, cops will be on their way, and I can't leave until I take him down.

She trained the gun on him for a second time, and again he evaded her, moving in a blur farther down the alley.

What the hell? He can't be human. Why would someone hire me to take down an android?

"Do you have any idea who I am?" Ra demanded. "You're out of your depth."

Ravenna charged toward him, her weapon raised. As Ra surged forward in an attempt to slip past her, Ravenna swung out her leg, focusing all her energy on tripping him.

Ra stumbled but did not fall. He caught Ravenna by the wrist, and her muscles screamed and strained as he used his grip on her to toss her toward the street. She threw out her free hand to catch herself. Her palm seared as it snagged on the sidewalk.

Ravenna forced herself to her feet and started into the alley after her target.

Enough. That's enough.

Ra laughed. He stood exactly where she had left him, holding her bracelet up toward the light of a streetlamp.

"If you give up this charade now, I'll let you li—"

Ravenna pulled the trigger, and her plasma bolt sank into Ra's abdomen.

"Not your call," she said flatly.

Ra frowned, looking downward. Blood spilled from his stomach onto the ground below him.

Without hesitation, Ravenna walked toward him, firing one shot after another. If he was an android, she knew one shot would not be sufficient.

An angry shout worked its way from Ra's throat as he launched himself toward her. Closing her eyes and bracing herself for the worst, she fired again.

Endless moments passed in an empty silence.

Ravenna forced her eyes open and let out a sharp breath. Ra lay at her feet, unmoving, a few of the bracelet's links spilling between his fingers and synthetic blood pooling in the new hole in his chest.

A scream cut through the night, followed by a succession of footsteps from the way the tourists had disappeared.

"Jo, call the police!" shouted a voice that sounded like the boy who'd walked past Ravenna's hiding place.

"Time's up," Ravenna breathed.

She turned on her heel and ran.

Ravenna glanced downward at the wrist where the bracelet had once hung. She then looked up into her aunt's eyes.

"After that, I had to disappear."

Clarisse inhaled deeply. "All right. Has it ever occurred to you how incredibly improbable it was that you managed to escape the nation's capital after committing a murder—with witnesses present—without even the slightest hint of government interference?"

Ravenna was silent. Yes, of course it had occurred to her. How could she not have considered it? But she had chosen not to dwell on what had made her escape possible and forced herself to be content with only the fact that she had succeeded.

"Would you like to know what happened immediately after you left the scene?"

Ravenna's heart missed a beat. "What?" she asked blankly.

Clarisse closed her eyes. "As soon as you were out of range, my people converged on the body and took it. They hid it away, fearing what would happen if it were ever found by the wrong people."

Still, Ravenna did not understand. She couldn't reconcile her aunt's words with what she knew, what she'd done.

"What are you saying?"

"You said yourself that you didn't know who hired you. That everything about the hit felt wrong. That's because it was." Clarisse stared pointedly at the table separating her from her niece as she continued. "You knew Ra wasn't human. You just didn't know what he was when you were hired."

"But you did." Ravenna's world was spinning as pieces clicked into place that shouldn't have reason to fit together. It shouldn't be possible. "You knew exactly what he was."

"Now remember yesterday, when I told you that the first group of Division androids was decommissioned. That was true, to an extent. We kept them locked away, hidden from the world. They weren't dangerous, that way. But eventually, they escaped, and we had no other option. We chose seven people to kill them before the androids could kill anyone else."

"It was you. All along, it was you. You hired me. You put my life on the line, knowing full well how easily he could have killed me!"

"Ravenna, it isn't that simple! I never meant—"

"No matter what you meant, I could be dead right now!" She was practically screaming, now. Her fury burst forth in an uncontrollable wave. She couldn't believe that her aunt had not only known that she'd turned to murder after leaving her home but that instead of intervening and pulling her back from the edge, Clarisse had used her as a hired gun to clean up the Division's mess.

"I did it to save you!" cried Clarisse. "Isabella agreed to pardon you for all the things you've done, when you succeeded!"

"If I succeeded," snarled Ravenna. "If Ra didn't slaughter me, like he did those people you sent him after." She pushed herself back from the table in disgust and turned away, starting toward the door.

"Ravenna, stop!"

Ravenna halted, staring furiously ahead. She felt a bit of blood pooling around her fingernails from her palms.

"You used me."

Without another word, she left the room, slamming the door behind her with such force that the walls shook.

Chapter Nine

The shards of glass and porcelain had already been swept up and thrown away, and Desi had turned the furniture back over to its rightful state. Her muscles had screamed in protest, but she hadn't paused in her work until it had been finished.

If she stopped moving, she was certain she would lose her composure.

She knew she should call her brother, but there was nothing he could do from West Point—West Point! It didn't seem real. She knew Ben would try to help her, but clearly legality wasn't a concern for whoever had broken into her apartment, and she doubted a restraining order would truly hold her pursuer back.

Was it Mia? She doubted Eddie could've slipped in without her noticing, but Mia was much more skilled at subterfuge. Still, Desi had no idea how she could have slept through glass breaking.

I must have had way more to drink than I remember.

She'd been pacing the floor of her living room for the better part of an hour since she'd finished cleaning. Her mind screamed at her to leave, to find somewhere to go that no one would anticipate. But the only place she could potentially run was LDE, and anyone who might be looking for her would know that was her next choice.

A frustrated cry burst from her lungs.

She'd thought her days of feeling helpless had been at an end, but it seemed they were just beginning.

As she paced, she caught sight of a square of paper she hadn't seen earlier sitting on one of the stools at her breakfast bar.

Frowning, she moved closer and lifted the paper from the seat. The words were written in a sharp, slanted hand she didn't recognize.

You aren't fit to lead LDE. Resign before you no longer have the choice.

Desi swayed on her feet and clutched the stool to steady herself.

The writing wasn't Eddie's, and unless he'd sent Mia to demolish her apartment and leave the note, she had no idea who could want her to abdicate her position enough to go this far. Her hands were suddenly cold, and they began to tremble.

At the sound of a honk from outside, Desi jumped. She ran to the window and looked outside, and she spotted Marley starting across the street, dark sunglasses and a headscarf presumably shielding her from a hangover.

Despite the gravity of her situation, Desi smiled at the sight of her friend. For a moment, she allowed herself to feel that she wasn't completely alone in Manhattan while her brother, Lila, and Ravenna were off chasing shadows.

A small black hovercar turned onto the street and rocketed forward along the bottom traffic lane. It swerved off the road and toward the young brunette with surgical precision.

Desi screamed.

The car slammed into Marley full-force, and she flew backward over its hood.

Eddie wove through the halls he'd become far too familiar with over the last several days for comfort, and eventually, he returned to his borrowed room. Since he'd tired of being restricted to the bedroom he was renting indefinitely, he'd taken to wandering Hathor's home when Mia was away. He occasionally turned on the telesense to find that the outside world still loathed him, and then he retreated into his shell. Into the house he was forbidden to leave until such time as Mia and her allies succeeded in the plan none of them had yet seen fit to tell him.

The living room and hallways were carpeted in grey, and the guest bedroom in which Eddie had been staying boasted a hardwood floor that he returned to when he wanted its chill to wake him and remind him that he was still alive.

He hadn't imagined that the steps he'd taken to secure his future would instead steal it from him.

"You've been pushed around for too long, Eddie. It's time for you to push back."

Mia leaned forward until her lips were barely an inch from his ear.

"Kill him."

Eddie wrenched himself away, leaping to his feet and taking several steps from the spot he had abandoned. He stared unblinkingly at the wall, unable to stand the sight of her. She was a spider, weaving a web with each word that he found increasingly difficult to escape. The words were undeserving of a response. He should leave. Leave, and not look back.

He didn't.

He leaned against the bedframe, focusing on the coolness that shot upward through his feet the longer he stood still on the wood. The headache that had accompanied the memory lingered, and he had almost become too accustomed to the pain to mind it. He was falling apart bit by bit, and the longer he stayed here, the more quickly he knew he would unravel.

"Can I get you anything? You're looking pale."

He turned to find Hathor standing in the doorway. She didn't move to approach him, and she was frowning, but she hadn't yet fled.

Mia had left the house in the early morning hours, as Eddie had learned when he'd gotten up to pace the first time. This time, he'd made a circuit around the house before returning to his room, and she still hadn't returned. He'd seen little of Horus, but that was always the case. Hathor's partner was even more reclusive than Eddie had become, it seemed, or perhaps he was out making plans as the rest of them often were.

Being the only human in a house full of androids was not the life Eddie had imagined for himself.

"No, thank you," Eddie said. "Unless you want to tell me what everyone's working on while I'm stuck here, that is."

Hathor's mouth twitched, and Eddie caught his mistake.

"I appreciate you letting me stay here very much," he said quickly. "I'm just... not used to being unable to go outside."

Hathor's expression softened somewhat, though she still resembled a flame-haired lioness prepared to strike. She stepped into the room and reclined against the wall beside the door.

"I'm not allowed to talk much about it. I'm sorry." The words sounded strange on her tongue, but he supposed it was simply because she wasn't used to them. He couldn't imagine she'd ever been one to apologize.

Eddie abandoned that line of questioning and moved instead to the overflowing bookshelf in the corner of his room. He ran his index finger along the spines of the books occupying it and found that very few of them had accumulated dust.

"Do you read often?" he asked her. "I've heard so little about your life."

Apart from Lila and Dana, the assistant to LDE's executives, Eddie hadn't had much contact with androids who were assimilated into the world. He designed them and arranged sales, but afterward, his contact with them was limited to business. He didn't know exactly what he'd expected Hathor's home to look like, but the fact that it was so... *normal* was a constant shock.

"When I'm not distracted by other things, yes," said Hathor.

"Which is your favorite?" Eddie gestured to the books.

Hathor scanned the shelves and bit her lip, and for a few moments, she was silent.

"*Gatsby,*" she said at last.

Eddie raised a brow. "Why's that? If you don't mind me asking, I mean."

"I think it's the most realistic. People are selfish and they take and take and don't care who they hurt. And I don't just mean humans—don't worry. We're just the same."

Before he could respond, Horus appeared in the doorway, his eyes narrowed as he looked from Hathor to Eddie and back again.

"We need to go," he said. "It's time. Mia's going to meet us there."

Hathor nodded and looked to Eddie. "You're welcome to anything in the fridge," she said.

A second later, she and Horus disappeared in a blur of red.

★

"I want you to know that while you're here, you're under the full protection of this organization, as well as the United States government."

Derek and Lila nodded in turn. Rachel took a deep breath and cracked her knuckles one at a time, debating how much was safe to tell them. *And legal,* she reminded herself.

"Before I say anything more, I need you to tell me how much you already know."

"We know about Mia," said Derek. "Why she was created. The things she's done."

Something in his expression told Rachel silently that he knew the truth about his parents' deaths. Her throat went dry, and she felt the need to reach out to him, to try to comfort him, as she knew all too well how deeply the loss of a parent cut. Her father had died before her mother's presidency, back when Isabella had still been a senator. Rachel still hadn't made peace with his passing.

"The circumstances that led to the Division's creation," Derek went on, "and that Mia wasn't the first android created for it."

Rachel tensed. "And where those prior to her are concerned, what were you told?"

It was Lila who answered. "That they went too far in their first mission and wiped out a town before they were decommissioned."

With measurable restraint, Rachel managed not to smile. Relief washed over her. She couldn't afford another security leak regarding those wretched androids that refused to disappear. If Lila and Derek didn't know they still existed, that was at least one small thing that had worked out in Rachel's favor.

"Yes, they were," she said. "It seems that you're already aware of most everything I had planned to tell you. I'll have to thank Clarisse for that later."

Lila raised an eyebrow, and Rachel suspected that her sarcasm had not gone unnoticed.

"Don't worry about Mia," said Rachel. "We'll take care of her. You're welcome to stay here until she's been apprehended, if you choose to."

"I have one concern."

Rachel turned her attention to Derek, who shifted his weight from one foot to the other. "Yes?"

"My sister. She's taking care of our company while I'm away, and Eddie has... personal interest in her, you could say."

I've seen the tabloids, Rachel thought, but she held her tongue. Still, the youngest Lawrence sibling was one loose end she had failed to consider. Rachel would need to send someone to retrieve her and bring her to West Point, if her safety was in question.

"I'm sure we can get her here and out of his—"

There was a knock at the door. The sound was insistent. Urgent.

"Come in," said Rachel quickly.

The door opened, and Kat stood outside, her eyes filled with a blend of sadness and fear.

"Did McNaire do something worse than we—?"

"Turn on the news," Kat said quietly, and Rachel's question died in her throat. She picked up the remote from the desk she leaned against and turned on the telesense mounted on the wall.

A reporter sat at a metallic blue news desk with her brown hair pulled into a tight bun. She stared over elliptical glasses into the camera.

"…that only one person in the house was killed," she was saying. "Police identified the body of Susan Rush, nurse to former President of the United States Isabella Hartley."

Images of Susan and Isabella appeared on the screen, side-by-side. Rachel's heart plummeted. She knew Susan. The freckled, kind-faced nurse had taken care of Rachel's mother for years, since the assassination attempt that had derailed Isabella's life. The image of Isabella was one from her last term in office several years earlier.

"According to police," the reporter continued, "Hartley was unharmed by the intruders, though emotionally shaken, as she heard the confrontation from down the hallway.

Authorities are uncertain as to why Rush was targeted while Hartley was spared." She paused. "The New York City fire department received quite a shock this morning when—"

Rachel turned off the telesense, her mind reeling, and closed her eyes. Silence filled the office.

Oh God. It's actually happening.

"I'm sorry," said Kat. "We'll need you to return to your rooms for the time being. We'll send for you as soon as possible."

Rachel heard movement throughout the room followed by dissipating footsteps.

"They're gone."

With a heavy sigh, Rachel looked to her cousin. Kat's lips were pressed into a thin line.

"What are we going to do?" she asked.

"Start the evacuation immediately. I want you and Blue Team protecting Ravenna. They're going to be after all of us, but if they discover she's here, they'll kill her first, and they won't leave her in one piece. She's the last one. Take Clarisse with you, and Derek and Lila."

Kat nodded quickly. "What are you going to do?"

"I have to find my mother."

"I'm going with you."

Rachel directed her attention to the doorway. Andrew stood just inside it, watching her with pain in his eyes.

"You should evacuate with the others," she said delicately. She only half-expected to survive the trip to retrieve her mother, and she would never forgive herself if harm befell Andrew.

He held her gaze, unwavering in his resolve. Rachel sighed, glancing between him and Kat, who appeared somewhat confused.

"Fine," said Rachel. "Let's go." She started toward the door, paused beside Kat, and embraced her for a long moment. "Be careful. Stay safe."

Rachel turned away as tears began to sting her eyes. She led Andrew from the room.

They had not yet reached the end of the hallway before the sirens began to wail.

Chapter Ten

Desi had no idea how long she had been screaming. Cameras flashed in the crowd surrounding her, and the EMTs fought to keep her still no matter how hard she struggled to run for Marley. She could no longer see her friend past the ambulance, but she had to reach her. She had to fix this.

"Do you know anyone who might have wanted to hurt Miss Kolakowski?"

"No." Desi was shaking from head to toe, and she set the cup of coffee the police officers had given her back on the table before she could burn herself with it.

Maybe that would wake me up.

She looked from Detective Masters to the uniformed officer sitting beside him across the table, a woman who was taking rapid notes on a tablet. The room where they sat was small and square, and Desi had seen enough on the telesense to know the mirror behind the officers was also a window.

"Do you think that this attack was in any way connected to your brother's murder?"

Desi stared at Masters, who watched her, stone-faced and accusatory.

"Do you think I had anything to do with either of them?" she countered, scowling.

"Answer the question, please, Miss Lawrence."

The door flew open, and Ben strode in, a briefcase in his hand.

"She will do no such thing," he snapped. "Interrogating my client without an attorney present, Detective? Desi, were you Mirandized?"

She shook her head and bit her inner cheek against the tears that wanted to break free. She'd never been so relieved to see anyone apart from the night at the warehouse.

"Inadmissible," said Ben simply, pausing beside where Desi sat and levelling a glare at Masters.

"Your client is not under arrest, McNaire," said the detective. "She's a witness to a hit-and-run."

"And you think her brother's death is an appropriate line of questioning?" Ben laughed flatly. "Nice try. Do you have anything else to ask her that actually pertains to the case at hand?"

Masters stared at Ben for several seconds, and then he shook his head.

Ben laid his hand on Desi's shoulder, and she jumped as an image of the day Eddie had crashed her lunch with Marley and Lucy sprang to her mind.

"Let's get out of here," Ben said softly.

Desi stood and followed him from the room and into the hallway outside, where she couldn't stop herself from throwing her arms around him and letting her tears run free at last.

"Thank you," she muttered. "I thought they were going to take me to the hospital to see her. Is Marley okay? Is she—?"

"I'm not sure," said Ben, hugging her gently before pulling back. "But I think it's time we talk about the parts you've told Ryder. I want to help you however I can, and I want to keep you away from whoever is doing all this and from the vultures." He shot a withering look at the door to the interrogation room.

"Okay." Desi swallowed and nodded.

She had no idea what Ben could do if Mia was indeed after her, but she would not go back to her apartment alone and she would not make the mistake of involving anyone else. Ben was already part of this twisted game whether he knew it or not, and Desi hoped that his father would assign a group of Secret Service agents to stay with him if necessary.

"Where to?" she asked.

Derek jumped as the high-pitched wail of the sirens assaulted his ears. His eyes wide, he turned to Lila, whose mouth hung open in an unspoken question. They had not yet reached the rooms they had been allotted when red lights began to flash along the tops of the slate-grey walls.

Derek surveyed the corridor. All around them, people began to run in every direction. Shoulders bumped Derek's and hands shoved him out of the way as West Point went mad.

Lila slid close to him, taking his arm. "What's going on?" she called over the din.

He shook his head through what felt like ten feet of water, unable to focus or think. He had no idea what could possibly have triggered the alarm other than a catastrophe the likes of which he was thoroughly unprepared to face.

"I have no idea," he called back to Lila. "Let's find out."

They took off at a run. Their footfalls were drowned out by the sirens and the shouts of the people around them.

A bang resounded through the hall.

Derek and Lila dove to the floor as the sound of concrete crashing into itself followed, and he pulled her close on reflex. Countless others had also flung themselves down in fear, their eyes searching for the source of the sound.

An enormous hole had appeared in the wall at the end of the hall Derek and Lila had just come from. A man and woman walked through the hole and the rubble surrounding it, their faces cold and pale in contrast with the woman's vibrant red hair and lips.

"Have you missed us?" called the man over the wail of the sirens. "We're home."

Derek's heart lurched. The blast hadn't seemed like that of a bomb—it looked like the pair of newcomers had caused it.

Androids.

He didn't recognize them, and he knew that none of LDE's androids had been designed to destroy.

The ones the Division created. They didn't decommission them. Is Mia with them?

Fear surged through him, and he pulled Lila to her feet. "Come on. We have to find Ravenna and get out of here."

A second bang entered the air, and Derek froze. He knew this sound. It was one that he had become far too familiar with over the last few weeks to be able to ignore. He looked up in time to see that the red-haired woman had raised her fist to catch the shot. She opened it to reveal a plasma burn.

"Run!" Lila breathed, her voice hitching on the word.

Derek sprinted forward, away from the newcomers and the shots that filled the air. Barely a second passed before the screaming began.

From the corner of his eye, Derek saw Lila turn her head toward the noise.

"Don't look back," he said. "Just keep going."

They thundered through the complex, and Derek was certain his stomach would roil its way out of his body. He hadn't been this frightened since the night he'd followed Lila's recently recovered memory to the warehouse to square off with his best friend.

Suddenly, a man in a military uniform flew through the air in front of them, crashing into the wall with a sickening crack.

"This way!" shouted Lila, pulling Derek in the direction opposite where the man had come from. Though his every fiber screamed at him not to, he chanced a glance down the other branch of the hallway.

Another pair of androids was tearing their way through a crowd of people, snapping necks and weapons with equal ease. The two were brown-skinned, the man's complexion a few shades darker than the woman's.

"*Where is she?*" the woman cried.

Derek wrenched his focus from the androids and poured all of his concentration into where he and Lila were running.

"Who do you think they're talking about?" Lila's voice was forcedly calm, though Derek knew her well enough to sense the terror beneath the surface.

"I don't know," he said.

In that moment, he felt utterly useless. He couldn't hope to fight the androids without a gun, and he doubted he would be able to pause long enough to search out one that hadn't been broken or crushed beneath rubble along with its owner. Lila possessed incredible strength and speed, and yet she was fighting her nature to remain with him, even at the cost of her own life.

In that moment, he knew he had to tell her.

"Lila, there's something I need you to know."

She looked at him, then, her face a composite of alarm and incredulity. "Derek, I don't think now is really the best—"

"Please. Please let me speak," he implored. "If something happens, I will have lost my only chance."

She nodded slowly, glancing between him and the overcrowded, overloud hall, which lost structural integrity by the second as more crashes and bangs filtered in from all sides and smoke poured through the air.

"Go ahead," she said.

"I love you," said Derek. "I have for longer than I can remember, but I've been denying it because I—" A blast from behind the pair sent them flying forward and crashing to the hard metal floor. Derek gritted his teeth against the pain of his shoulder slamming into the surface and pushed himself up again as Lila did the same beside him, and they ran. "I shouldn't have waited this long."

Shrieking, a group of suited people plowed their way between Derek and Lila as they ran in the opposite direction. Panic coursed through him until she reappeared at his side.

"Derek, I—"

"Go on," said a smooth female voice from behind Derek.

His heart jumped into his throat.

He turned to see the female android he'd just witnessed breaking soldiers' necks standing inches from him. Her irises were bright emerald, and they didn't look remotely as human as those belonging to LDE's creations.

"I'm interested to see where this goes," she said, raising a brow.

"Don't play with them, Bastet."

The dark-skinned man had appeared at her side, and he was scowling. He reached out and grabbed Derek by the throat.

Gasping and spluttering, Derek struggled to pry the man's fingers free. An instant later, Lila stood between him and his attacker. She twisted the man's arm until he released his hold on Derek and rounded on her, his eyes—mirrors of his companion's—wide with shock.

"One of us?" he asked, a hint of amusement coloring his tone.

As Derek rubbed at his aching throat and backed toward the wall, Lila scoffed.

"Not even close," she said.

The woman called Bastet charged at her and grabbed her by the shoulder, slamming her hard against the wall.

"You'll wish you were," she snarled.

Lila drove her fist hard into Bastet's stomach, sending her flying backward into the wall a few feet from where Derek stood. Lila hissed, and Derek realized a moment too late that Bastet had swiped at her at the moment of impact and left four deep scratches across Lila's clavicle.

Synthetic blood pooled along the lines and dappled the ripped cloth of her shirt.

Bastet took a step toward Lila, glaring daggers.

"Why them over us?" she asked. "What can they give you?"

The sound of gunfire from the right drew Derek's attention once again, and he looked up as Bastet deflected a plasma bolt into the wall. She locked eyes with her companion.

"Anubis," she said simply.

Without further discussion, the two of them charged toward their attackers in a blur, and Derek watched in horror as they intersected a group of men and women in camouflage partially obscured by the smoke pouring down the hall.

A round of fire followed instantly, intermingled with screams. A few moments later, smoke was all Derek could see from the direction in which the androids had gone.

"This way, come on!"

Derek's head whipped toward the voice. Kat stood a few yards down to his left, looking flushed and furious. Behind her stood Casey, Charlie, and Lex, their guns trained on where Bastet and Anubis had vanished.

Lights began to dance around the edges of Derek's vision as he ran. He had nearly begun to question his physical state and his sanity when he processed how pungent the smell of smoke had become.

He took another glance down the hallway to his right, and his fears were confirmed.

West Point was ablaze. Flames leapt along the walls, consuming everything in their path.

"Where's Ravenna?" Lila cried, grabbing Derek's hand.

"Outside with Abigail," called Kat, "waiting for us."

Immense relief crashed over Derek. At least one person he cared for was safe.

"What about Rachel?" This, too, came from Lila.

Kat was silent for a long moment. "I think she got out. She and Andrew were going to find Rachel's mother."

"They'll be okay, Kat," insisted Lex. "They're both trained and both smart. They'll be fine."

Kat nodded. She did not, however, appear convinced.

"There!" yelled Casey. "Through that door!"

Despite his exhaustion, Derek pushed himself forward. He could not stop running if they were to survive. He felt suspended in time, moving forward in a circle, unable to gain ground. His grip on Lila's hand was the only thing keeping him from falling over the edge.

The group reached the door. Derek and Kat rammed into it, but the only result was the pain that splintered up and down Derek's arm from the point of contact.

"Got it."

Lex stepped to the side and took aim at the door. He deployed a series of shots into its frame until he'd blasted it off its hinges, and then with a strong kick, he knocked it free. It crashed to the ground outside.

"Let's move," he said.

As the blaze engulfed the remainder of the hallway, Derek, Lila, and the unit known as Blue Team fled.

Chapter Eleven

Rachel and Andrew's footfalls resonated through the empty air as they ran down the street, leaving the burning building far behind them. The only other sound was their breathing, which had grown heavy after the endless expanse of minutes they had spent working to escape the invasion. Rachel had decided that running would attract less attention, if everyone else was fleeing in a mass of cars. She had enough contacts in the vicinity to ensure that when they were far enough from West Point, they could procure a vehicle of their own.

She couldn't believe the androids had moved on them in daylight. She supposed they could have simply been working against expectations, and if so, their plan had succeeded. She had anticipated a strike by night, and she had been misled.

"Where are we going?" asked Andrew.

"Right now, let's concentrate on forward," said Rachel breathlessly.

He nodded, and they continued on as her lungs ached. She had caught only a glimpse of two of the invaders, but that had been enough to allow her to recognize them with ease. Bastet and Anubis. Rachel knew that the others would not be far behind; Osiris, Isis, Hathor, and Horus were probably somewhere within the base, as well.

The thought made her almost physically ill. It was poetic, in a way. The Division was responsible for its own undoing. Had it not created these androids—along with Ra, their fallen leader—its base of operations would not be in flames.

If only the seven hired assassins had succeeded in destroying these menaces all those years earlier. If only the androids could have been stopped before they had become vengeful as well as dangerous.

"If we can get a few blocks farther," she told Andrew, "I know someone who will let us borrow a car. Then we can find my mom."

"Not so fast."

Someone blindsided Rachel, hitting her in the back of the head and sending her flying to the ground. She caught herself before her face could make contact and shoved herself up onto her elbows as the world around her blurred. Straining her eyes in an effort to focus her vision, she saw that Andrew had been flung down the street.

"No!" Rachel shouted.

Andrew produced his plasma gun and quickly stood, taking aim at something Rachel could not see. Suddenly, in a blur of motion, a copper-haired man shot toward Andrew. The former pulled the latter to his feet and twisted his arm behind his back. A sickening snap echoed through the air, and the gun clattered to the ground.

Horus.

A slender hand grasped Rachel by the throat and lifted her roughly upward. Her feet dangled several inches off the ground as she gasped for air.

"Hello, Rachel."

"H—Hathor—"

"Where is the surviving assassin?" the android demanded, her lips set in a snarl.

"I—I don't—"

"Don't lie to me!" Hathor tightened her grip on Rachel's neck, and Rachel gagged. "You're their leader. You have to know."

Tears stung Rachel's eyes, and she glanced to Andrew, whose face was contorted in pain. Horus had not relinquished his grip on Andrew's arm.

"Let—him—go," Rachel choked. *"Please.* Take—me."

Hathor turned to face the others, swinging Rachel along without effort as she smirked.

"Patience, Hartley. You'll pay for what you've done. And so will everyone else involved in your games. It's time for us to have what's ours. We want our lives. If we have to take them, so be it."

Horus picked up the gun and pointed it at Andrew.

"No!" Rachel had become disoriented, and she had no idea how long she could continue to fight. "All right. I'll—take you—to her."

Hathor released Rachel, dropping her to the pavement. Rachel gasped, her hands flying to her aching neck.

"That's more like it."

The silence in the car was unnerving, and Derek couldn't stand it any longer.

"Who were they?"

He stared at Ravenna's shoulder. His car had been commandeered by Abigail Knight, who hadn't said a word since the group had left West Point, and with his ability to drive stolen away, Derek had elected to sit in the back with Lila. Ravenna knew more than she had told him—of that much, he was certain. He'd barely seen her since their arrival at West Point, and he knew she must've spoken with her aunt. Abigail certainly knew far more than any of them, but Derek had been stonewalled by Rachel too many times to expect answers from her lieutenant.

"If you think I know," said Ravenna, "you've been misled."

"Of the three of us, you know the most about the Division. The people that broke in were obviously more than human."

"Androids," said Lila quietly. Derek nodded.

Ravenna closed her eyes. "If I had to guess, they were probably the original Division androids. The ones that were supposed to have been decommissioned."

Abigail turned the car sharply, and Derek clung to the handle above the door to keep himself steady.

"What?"

Ravenna refused to turn toward him. "Apparently, they escaped. The Division hired a group of assassins to take them out, and the plan backfired. Badly."

"What happened to the assassins?" asked Derek, though he was sure he knew.

Ravenna paused. "They were killed."

Lila dropped her face into her hand. "How many deaths is the Division responsible for?"

Derek knew the question was rhetorical, but still he shook his head. "Too many," he said. His thoughts had grown cynical. *And these are the people responsible for keeping us safe. How can we trust them? Yes, they've done what they can to protect us. But if it comes down to it, can we really be sure that we're on the same side?*

"You should try to call Desi," suggested Ravenna. "She's going to need time to pack."

He nodded absently and produced his cell phone. He called his sister's number, and the ringing on the other end persisted until the tone was replaced by an automated greeting.

"It's Desi. Leave a message and I'll get back to you."

Derek frowned. Where could she be? If she were at the office and saw him calling, wouldn't she assume it was urgent, given the way their last conversation had gone?

"Where are we going?" asked Lila, breaking the silence in the car.

"Somewhere safe," said Abigail.

Derek wanted to scream at her refusal to give them any semblance of an actual answer. He was spared the need to comment when Ravenna's phone rang.

"Hello?" she mumbled.

After a moment, she nodded.

"Is she in danger?" she asked. A few beats passed in silence, and then she spoke again. "Hold on." She lowered the phone and turned in her seat to face Derek. "Kat wants to pick up Desi immediately."

Derek tensed. He'd known retrieving his sister was part of the plan, but the fact that Kat was concerned twisted his stomach. "Are they after her, too?"

"I don't know. But she would be safer with us."

Derek wanted more than anything to believe that his sister would be safe if she were to join their group. But he didn't even feel safe, and the thought of subjecting his sister to a situation that he didn't trust deeply unsettled him. Still, he didn't want to leave her alone if the band of androids planned to turn their sights on her, and he still had no idea where Eddie and Mia were.

He nodded stiffly. "I'll keep trying to call her. I haven't had any luck yet."

"He's trying," said Ravenna into the phone. Her tone was flat, and after a brief pause, she spoke again. "I've heard enough. More than enough. More than one person can be asked to handle in such a short amount of time. So, save it."

She hung up and then glanced toward Derek and Lila.

"Clarisse," she said simply.

When Desi entered the tall, wood-floored foyer of Ben's home, she hadn't yet stopped shaking. She didn't know if she ever would. The image of Marley flying over the hood of the car replayed in her mind on a sick loop. Each time, Desi grew closer to shattering.

"Would you like something to eat or drink?" asked Ben. He shrugged off his suit jacket and hung it on the rack beside the wall.

The impulse to ask for alcohol flicked through her mind, but she ignored it.

"If you have any coffee," she said instead, "that would be wonderful, thank you."

Their eyes met, and Ben frowned slightly.

"How much have you had over the past week?"

"I… don't know. A few cups a day."

"Are you sleeping? Trying to keep yourself awake isn't healthy."

She sighed. "I sleep. When I can't stand it anymore. But I'd rather stay awake than see what I do when I let myself dream."

Ben's frown deepened. He led her into the living room and to the leather sofa, and he settled into the chair beside it. An immense telesense dominated the wall opposite them, and to Desi's left was a small bar that looked far more appealing than she wanted to admit.

"I'm not a psychiatrist," said Ben. "But I'd like to talk with you as a friend, if that's okay."

A small laugh that bordered on hysterical burst from Desi's throat.

"You've seen what happens to my friends," she said quietly. "All Marley did was answer my call to come see me, and some asshole hit her with a car! You don't want me to tell you anything, Ben. Me being here has already probably painted a target on your head the size of Texas."

"If I make a call to my dad, he can have Secret Service people here within the hour. I really don't think I'm in any danger."

"You don't understand," Desi whispered. "You don't know what they can do."

"Then help me understand."

He wrapped her hand in both of his own, and she searched his earnest green eyes for a sign of hesitation. She found none, and she let out a heavy breath.

"Eddie wasn't alone in the warehouse," she said. "There was an android with him that I didn't know about until she rushed him out of the building after Ravenna shot him. According to my brother, the military commissioned her to serve as a replacement for soldiers."

Desi paused. As she'd spoken, Ben's face had drained of color, and she watched him, her brows drawn.

"What is it?" she asked.

"The Division?" he breathed.

Desi's stomach lurched.

"You know about it?"

"My father is the president, Desi. And that organization is probably the thing he hates most in this country. Hartley started it when she was in office, and he's been trying to shut it down ever since. He was her Secretary of Defense, and the Division drove a wedge between them that never went away. I..." Ben ran a hand through his hair as a look of embarrassment crept onto his face. "I begged him to let me join it for years until I realized it was never going to happen. I thought I could actually do something to help America there."

"Derek and Lila and Ravenna are with them now. Ravenna—her aunt is Clarisse—"

"Clarisse *Mitchell*?"

"Yes," Desi said quickly.

"She and Hartley started the whole thing. They commissioned a wave of androids that went terribly wrong and killed a bunch of people."

Desi could sit still no longer. She pushed herself to her feet and began to pace the wooden floor.

"And then they commissioned her," she said. "Because they failed. But if they—"

Her gaze landed on a photoscroll on the wall above the bar, which projected an image of a group of people in suits standing outside Ben's law firm. The face of the auburn-haired woman standing at the image's right caught Desi's eye, and she moved closer to examine it.

Her heart leapt into her throat.

In the photo, standing next to Ben, was Mia.

"You know her?" she asked blankly.

Ben was on his feet in an instant and made his way to her side. He glanced to the photo and blinked, looking puzzled.

"Who?"

Desi tapped the picture of Mia's face, and Ben nodded.

"Mia Warren," he said. "My secretary."

Desi whipped around to stare at him, her mouth hanging open. Her mind spun at a hundred miles per hour, and she couldn't understand.

"That's her," she said. "That's the android Eddie made for the Division."

"She's..." Ben's eyes widened as he frowned. "She's been working for me for..."

"How long?" Desi pressed.

"A couple of weeks. Her credentials were outstand—"

"Faked," she said flatly. "Warren was Eddie's mother's maiden name."

Ben blinked and backed toward his chair, sinking into it and dropping his head into his hands.

"How could I let something like that get past me?"

"She's probably spying on you," said Desi. "Or... oh, damn it, does she know you're working my case?"

He looked up at her, then, panic in his eyes.

"I'm so sorry, Desi. I had no idea who she was. No idea." He pulled in a long breath. "Let me call my father. I'll get security here as soon as—"

A high-pitched ring interrupted his words, and he pulled his phone from his pocket.

"McNaire," he said into the receiver.

He was silent for several seconds, and then he went even paler, which Desi hadn't thought possible.

"Thank you," he said at last before laying the phone on the arm of his chair. He stared blankly at the floor.

"What is it?" Desi asked.

"I... I'm so sorry. Marley... they did everything they could."

A choked sob worked its way up from Desi's lungs, and she doubled over, clutching her knees.

"This is my fault," she muttered. "It's all my fault. I shouldn't have called her. It's my fault."

She felt Ben's arm around her, and she couldn't stop herself from leaning on him, clutching his shoulders as her sobs shook her body. He guided her to the sofa and embraced her silently, and she let herself weep until she lost track of how many minutes had passed.

I have to go, she thought at last, doing her best to pull herself into the present. *I can't let anyone else get hurt because of me. I have to leave Manhattan.*

"Can you—" She sniffed and squared her shoulders, attempting to string together a coherent sentence. "Before your dad's people get here, can you take me by my place so that I can pick up some things?"

"Of course," he said, nodding. "I'd be happy to."

The thought of what she would have to do turned Desi's blood to ice. But if she needed to leave to draw Mia away with her, she hoped Ben would forgive her, in the end.

Chapter Twelve

Clarisse glared at the list of names projected above the holofile on her desk. She'd been studying the list for the better part of an hour, and no matter how she tried to shake the beginnings of a bad idea from her mind, she couldn't entirely rid herself of it.

The words "Known Assassins' Guilds" glared ominously up at her from the top of the readout hovering several inches above the smooth, flat silver screen. Clarisse flicked the right edge of the projection, and its title disappeared to give way to more items on the list as the cursor scrolled downward.

I don't want the help of any of these. Caedis, Laurea, Viperae… Clarisse shook her head. They can't be trusted. How did we get to the point that we can't stop the guilds, anyway? How did we lose that much power?

As she surveyed the names, she fiddled absently with the small chain links of the gold bracelet on her left wrist. She remembered the day she'd given one just like it to her niece, who had, as a child, wanted to follow in her footsteps and work for the government. Clarisse had brought Ravenna along on several visits to the White House when she'd been Senior Advisor to President Hartley, and now that she had been reassigned to head an organization that was far more trouble than it was worth, Clarisse found her thoughts returning to her niece again.

Would she want to be part of this? Could I even tell her I was the one hiring her? I would have to arrange something. I'd be drawing attention to her; I have to make sure she's protected.

Clarisse skimmed the list for a few seconds longer without seeing a word projected, and then she pulled in a quick breath and pushed herself backward from her desk. She slid to her feet, and her chair bobbed slightly where it hovered just above the floor at the loss of her weight. She rolled her shoulders backward, smoothed out her skirt, and kept her hold on the holofile as she strode out of her office and down the corridor.

The walls on either side of her path were lined with paintings that had been considered antique for hundreds of years; former leaders stared somberly out at the hallway. Clarisse refused to allow her eyes to linger on any of them for too long. She doubted most of them would have allowed their nation to be put into this position in the first place.

When she reached the door she sought, Clarisse pulled in a long breath and knocked.

"Yes?" called the voice of President Isabella Hartley from the other side.

"It's Clarisse, ma'am."

"Come in."

Clarisse pushed open the door and entered the Oval Office. Isabella sat at her desk, her hands folded and her long red hair pulled back into a tight bun.

"Have you had any luck solving our problem?" Isabella asked.

"Somewhat, Madam President," said Clarisse. "As you know, my niece is… ah…"

"She's run into trouble with the law?" Isabella supplied.

Clarisse's cheeks burned. "Yes, ma'am."

"Where is she, now? Still in Chicago? Did she align with one of the guilds?"

"No. She works alone." Clarisse pulled in a long breath and let it out again. "Madam President," she continued, "I've thought about this for weeks, since your proposal that we enlist a guild to take the Seven down. I think we would stand a better chance of remaining off the radar if we hire lone assassins. People who won't draw attention because they choose not to be found even by others like them. If they succeed, word won't spread, and if they fail—" The words died in Clarisse's throat. She refused to allow herself to picture Ravenna failing at such a dangerous game.

When Clarisse said nothing for a few moments, Isabella spoke again.

"You want her to be one of them?" she asked, raising a red brow.

Clarisse swallowed, her fingers moving to her bracelet on reflex. "I know Ravenna's capable," she said. "I only waited this long because I worry about her. I decided I trust her to do it and keep herself safe."

Isabella glanced to the photoscroll on her desk. Though it was facing away from Clarisse, she knew it contained a series of images of Isabella's family programmed to play on a loop.

Isabella, no doubt, was thinking about her daughter, who was Ravenna's age.

"In exchange, I'd want her pardoned," said Clarisse. "For everything. Off the record."

Isabella's eyes flicked back to meet Clarisse's, her mouth pressed into a tight line.

"I knew it would be something like that," Isabella muttered.

"She's made mistakes. I just... I think she can change—can stop going down this path. And when she does, I want her to be able to put it all behind her. Please, Madam President. I've done everything you've asked of me."

I gave up my real job as your advisor to head the Division. And now the blood of everyone those androids have killed is on my hands, *Clarisse wanted to say.*

Isabella watched her, and Clarisse kept all her focus on remaining still and slowing the thrum of her pulse. At last, Isabella sighed.

"Fine," she said. "An unofficial pardon in exchange for one of them being silenced." She held out her hand. "You have my word."

Relief crashed over Clarisse, and she grabbed Isabella's hand a bit more firmly than she'd intended.

"Thank you, ma'am. Thank you."

Clarisse stared out the window of the black SUV she had entered with Blue Team. She had the back row of the vehicle to herself, and while that only put her a foot or so from where Charlie and Casey sat in the second row, she felt miles away from everyone, too far out to sea to retain sight of the shore.

Clarisse surveyed Ra's unblinking emerald eyes. She'd always been unsettled by how inhuman they looked in each of the Seven.

Why couldn't our engineers at least try to make them pass for normal?

She sighed and pulled the white sheet covering the lower half of Ra's body up to conceal his face, as well.

"As promised," said Isabella's voice from behind her, "I will ensure that no one is looking for Ravenna."

Clarisse turned away from the dead android and faced Isabella, who stood in the chrome-plated lab's doorway.

"Thank you, ma'am," Clarisse said quietly.

Isabella nodded. "And this was with him."

She reached out and dropped Ravenna's golden bracelet into Clarisse's hand.

She's fine. She succeeded, and she's fine.

Still, Clarisse's mouth went dry, and she slipped the bracelet into her pocket without a word.

Through the fabric of her pants, her fingers brushed the cold metal of the bracelet lodged at the bottom of her pocket. It was the twin to the one she wore on her left wrist, and it had been wrapped in Ra's hand when Division agents had recovered his body.

Clarisse had meant to return it to Ravenna the next time they met. Over the fourteen years since she'd last seen her nice, Clarisse had lost her nerve while Ravenna had gained her own. She wasn't likely to forgive her aunt for her deception anytime soon, no matter how well-intentioned it had been.

"We need to go to Washington."

The words were Kat's from the front seat, and they were barely loud enough for Clarisse to hear.

"We'll meet with our agents stationed there and come up with a decent plan. Besides, there are far more places to hide there than in the immediate area."

"I'm not arguing with you," said Lex. "We should probably contact McNaire."

"We can draw straws," said Casey with a chuckle.

"Let's get a little bit farther away, first," said Kat. "We need to make sure we aren't being followed. And keep trying Rachel. Please."

Casey nodded and held her phone up to her ear.

Clarisse sighed and looked out the window again, her fingers still tracing the outline of the bracelet.

Desi's heart pounded nauseatingly as she and Ben approached her apartment's front door. She'd told him she just needed to gather some things for their trip to meet his father, wherever that led, and guilt gnawed at her with each passing second. She'd never been one to lie, and she hated how much easier it became the more she found herself pressured into it by circumstance.

More than anything, she wanted to call for help. She wanted Derek to know where she was and exactly what was happening, and she wanted Lucy. The two of them and Marley had been inseparable in college, and now that they had lost Marley, she knew Lucy would need someone just as much as she did.

But she couldn't call her, and she couldn't call Derek. She needed to leave Ben's company as soon as humanly possible.

She unlocked the door and hesitated for the span of a breath on the threshold.

The apartment was dark and silent.

"Lights," she ordered, and they flicked on to illuminate the apartment in the same state in which she'd left it upon rushing out onto the street for Marley, at least from what she could see. She let out a quiet breath and led Ben into the living room. "Make yourself at home," she said. "For what it's worth."

She knew they were supposed to be stopping in for only a few minutes, and she doubted he would want to waste time with a drink or a tour.

"Thank you," he said. He started for the sofa and paused in his tracks, looking to her. "Is there anything I can do to help?"

Desi shook her head. "No, but thanks. I'll be able to find everything quickly."

Ben nodded and settled onto the sofa, and Desi left him to rush into her bedroom. She closed the door and leaned back against it, her eyes closed tightly.

You can do this. You have to. It's the only way to make sure he stays safe.

If her plan worked correctly, she would have a decent head start before he realized she wasn't where she was supposed to be.

She rushed to the closet and pulled her clothes free indiscriminately, tossing them onto her unmade sheets. From the bottom of her closet, she dug out the large, black leather purse she'd gotten from Lila for her last birthday. She tossed the purse onto her bed and shoved shirts, pants, and dresses into it without pausing to gauge whether they suited the weather. By her rough estimate, she'd gathered enough for a couple of weeks, and she hoped that was long enough either for the stress to die down or for her to find somewhere decently permanent to stay.

Desi hurried into her bathroom, the purse swinging at her wrist, and threw in every bit of makeup and every toiletry within her reach. She didn't have the luxury of time to think deeply on what she would need, and she had always leaned toward the side of the over-prepared.

When she'd finished, she deposited the purse on her bed and inhaled before returning to the living room.

"Close to ready," she told Ben, who was examining the photoscroll on the end table. It cycled through pictures of Desi's family and friends, and at the moment, it showed her standing with her parents years earlier on the steps of the U.S. Capitol.

"That's good," said Ben with a smile. He seemed to be trying hard to keep himself calm, and she could only imagine the fallout that they would face if they were to go to President McNaire and explain the situation with the Division. From what Ben had said, his father would likely be furious. Another twinge of guilt shot through Desi at the thought that she was going to leave him to face his father alone.

She rushed into the kitchen and rooted through the cabinets, pulling out bags of chips and boxes of protein bars and whatever else was within reach. Packing food was excessive for the plan she was supposed to be following; she was certain Ben would find it odd considering that they would likely be provided for by his father's people. But in truth, she had no idea when she would find somewhere stable to stay and find decent food.

"Won't be long," she said as she brushed through the living room on the way back to her bedroom. She closed the door behind her and locked it. "Changing clothes," she called by way of explanation, and then she shoved the food into her bag, hoisted it onto her shoulder, and unlocked the door to her balcony.

As quietly as possible, she slipped outside and closed the door behind her. She scanned the area to find the fire escape just to the right of the balcony's railing. Pulling in a steadying breath, she climbed over the rail and landed on the metal surface beside it with a clang.

Go. Just go, she ordered herself, trying hard to ignore the fear and self-loathing welling up within her as she descended the fire escape toward the ground.

Chapter Thirteen

Kat paced the parking lot while Charlie filled up the gas tank. Derek had already filled up his car and appeared to have wrestled control of the wheel away from Abigail, whom Kat could see through the windshield sitting in the passenger seat with her arms folded irritably.

With a sigh, Kat pulled out her phone. She knew she couldn't stall any longer.

She sighed as she mentally prepared herself, but before she could will the phone to call President McNaire, it rang, and his name blared across the screen.

Shit.

She held the phone to her ear. "Yes, sir?"

"What the hell are you people doing?" McNaire demanded. "What happened at West Point?"

Kat closed her eyes and pinched the bridge of her nose. "It was the androids, sir. The original ones. I didn't see Mia with them, but she may have been. The place was a madhouse."

"How many casualties?"

Kat's stomach lurched. She realized, then, that she had no idea. She hadn't stayed long enough to see who had made it out alive, and in the chaos, she hadn't received any reports from agents since the attack. She supposed that the other agents would've tried to report to Rachel and not her.

"I don't know, sir."

"That's unacceptable. Get me a status report within the hour."

"I will."

"And are there civilians with you?"

Kat looked toward Derek's car. She caught sight of him scowling down at his phone and then glanced to Lila and Ravenna in the backseat.

"Due to exigent circumstances, yes," she said.

The back of her mind prickled with discomfort at the thought that McNaire had already known.

"Get them and yourselves to Washington as soon as humanly possible," he ordered. "My son has informed me that Mia has killed a young woman in Manhattan."

Kat froze in her pacing so quickly that she nearly slipped on the pavement.

"Who?" she muttered, looking once again to Derek through the window.

"Marlena Kolakowski."

Relief crashed over Kat, and it was instantly replaced by sickening guilt. Though she'd feared for Derek's sister, the fact that Mia had gone far enough to kill anyone was a catastrophe. Blue Team had failed in its mission to neutralize her before she caused further harm.

"I'm sorry," she whispered.

"We'll discuss it later," said McNaire sharply. "My son also told me that he was in the process of escorting Desdemona Lawrence here for protection when she disappeared. The girl was killed in a hit-and-run outside Desdemona's home."

"Wait, disappeared?" Kat spluttered. Charlie paused while climbing into the car to shoot her a puzzled look, and Kat waved her hand dismissively. Charlie shrugged and entered the car.

"Watch your tone, Kathleen."

Kat let out a quiet sigh and turned away from the cars and toward the building. Through the glass doors, she saw oblivious citizens shopping at a leisurely pace for fountain soda and candy.

So lucky.

"We have to find her, sir. This is our mess, and we will clean it up."

"Yes, you will."

The line went dead.

Desi maneuvered through Manhattan's streets indecisively. She hadn't decided where exactly she was running away to, and as she drove east and then west and then east again, she debated her options. She couldn't run to family or friends, if she wanted them to remain out of Mia's crosshairs. She'd never considered abandoning her life and everyone in it, which meant she had never thought about where she would go if she suddenly had to escape. At last, she made her way out of the city and into the less-populated areas beyond, and traffic thinned.

Having observed that loud music helped to take her mind off the hole forming in her heart, she had turned up her speakers to a nearly deafening volume, and they blasted synthpop and mind-numbing bass through her ears.

This is wonderful. After everything, after working so hard to pull my life together, here I am without a clue.

She glanced to the passenger seat and the large purse she'd stuffed with as many toiletries and articles of clothing as she could manage. She'd estimated that it held enough for two weeks or so, though she couldn't be sure she'd grabbed everything she needed in her rush to leave her apartment.

As she returned her eyes to the road, she pulled in a gasp so sharp her lungs stung.

Mia stood at the center of the freeway, silhouetted in the dying light of dusk.

Desi slammed on the brakes and yanked the wheel to the left in an attempt to miss her. A horrified glance out the right window—which was now facing Mia and the road ahead—revealed that the android was not trying to avoid the inevitable collision.

Instead, she stood her ground, extending an arm.

Desi closed her eyes and braced for impact.

Instead of knocking Mia over or fazing her in any fashion, the car crunched and bent around her outstretched arm. The metal of the passenger side wrapped around her, and she halted the car's motion with her other hand.

In one fluid movement, she flung the car away from her.

Desi screamed. The sound was drowned out by her speakers as the car flew through the air, end over end. Her forehead smacked against the steering wheel. As the car came crashing down to the road, the music ground to a halt, and Desi was left with the screech and crunch of metal. The car landed on its right side, rolling over twice before coming to a halt on its left.

After an endless moment of disjointed oblivion, Desi's eyes fluttered open, and she gasped. The sudden movement sent a shockwave of blinding pain from her ribcage just beneath her right breast. Struggling for air, she scanned the car. The windows and windshield had been shattered. Her head rested on the pavement among glass shards. Her body felt like a singular bruise, and her skin was lined with cuts and scrapes. Her pulse raged against her skull, and her forehead throbbed from the impact with the steering wheel. Still, the pain was nothing compared to that shooting from her ribs. She looked down toward its source.

A large chunk of glass that had fallen from the passenger window was lodged into her side. The cut felt deep, and her shirt was soaked through with blood. She caught her breath, which she immediately realized was a mistake when her agony increased tenfold.

What the hell?

The sound of ripping metal pierced the air for the second time. Desi looked toward the noise to watch as the passenger door was rent away from the car. She twisted farther into herself in a feeble effort to escape, but she knew it would do nothing for her.

She was trapped.

Mia tossed the door aside, not a scratch visible on her body, and stared down at Desi.

"Trying to run away, now?"

Desi said nothing. Mia rolled her eyes.

"Fine. Have it your way."

She reached into the car and snapped the seatbelt restraining Desi with one flick of her wrist. She then grabbed Desi's arm and lifted her roughly from the vreckage. With a sharp hiss, Desi did her best to relax and let herself be pulled free.

Mia deposited her onto the pavement, but her legs gave way immediately, her knees buckling beneath her as she stumbled downward. Mia held her aloft by the elbow and hoisted her up again with a grip that felt like a tourniquet.

"He's just going to have to realize how much of a liability you are," the android mumbled.

He?

When Desi's strained mind finally caught up to what Mia was saying, her eyes widened.

"What?" she breathed, trying to inject sarcasm into her tone despite her terrible state. "He didn't put you up to it?"

Mia reached for the glass shard embedded in Desi's side and ripped it free, tossing it across the street as Desi cried out in white-hot agony. Her hands flew on instinct to the injury, and nausea rolled through her stomach as she felt the sticky warmth of blood beneath her fingers. She glanced down at the jagged edges of the wound and swallowed the bile that surged upward at the sight.

"So fragile," said Mia. "Pathetic. But I guess you didn't die on impact like Mom and Dad, so that's something."

Desi stared at the android, her mind rejecting the words she had just heard.

"What?" she muttered.

"Oops," said Mia flatly. "Guess you didn't know."

Tears bit at Desi's eyes, but she fought them back, unwilling to show this woman any further weakness. Perhaps the words were just an unwarranted attack and were as false as Mia's remorse for them. She shot Mia a scathing look, which the android ignored. Mia scooped Desi from her feet and threw her over her shoulder, and without another word, she shot forward at a run that was quicker than Desi had ever moved.

Derek followed Kat around the corner of the gas station, doing his best to ignore the prickling of discomfort rising within him. He glanced back at his car, where Lila and Ravenna remained with Abigail, before they were out of sight.

"I needed to approach you about something personally," said Kat as she halted. Her face was draped in shadows as the sun descended, and it gave her a far more sinister look than suited her. "I've just spoken with the president. His son is your family's lawyer, isn't he?"

Derek nodded. He'd never had many dealings with Ben, but he knew his parents had held him in high esteem.

"Apparently he's been working closely with your sister on the Dodson case. He also contacted the president out of worry for Desdemona."

Derek's thoughts flicked to the phone in his pocket and the dozen calls he'd made to Desi that had gone unanswered.

"Why is that?" he asked, his throat suddenly tight and dry.

"Apparently Mia has killed someone named Marlena."

Derek leaned heavily against the side of the building, his palm flat against the metal wall to steady himself as his knees quaked at this news.

"Kolakowski?" he asked halfheartedly. He knew the answer already, but still he felt obligated to confirm that one of his sister's best friends had been killed.

Damian and Marley within a matter of weeks. She's going to fall apart. And I'm not there for her.

"Yes," said Kat. "If I may ask, what's the connection?"

"She's one of Desi's friends."

Kat sighed. "She was killed in a hit-and-run outside your sister's place."

Derek closed his eyes. He wanted to shut out the news, shut out the shattering of the world around him. He'd seen Marley at birthday parties and in tabloids with her face beside his sister's. He'd known her for the better part of six years. She'd been one of the most vibrant people he'd known—full of life and constantly dancing and dragging Desi into the next bad idea. The thought that she had been stricken and left to die made him ill.

"The word is that it was Mia."

Derek froze. He returned his focus to Kat, scowling in disgust and horror.

"Where is Desi?" he asked.

"We don't know."

"You don't know?" Derek demanded. This was unacceptable. The Division was incapable of even the most basic detainment of its creations. It couldn't stop them from striking out blindly against innocents, and after what he'd seen at West Point, the thought of Mia being anywhere near his sister was too much to bear.

"Ben McNaire was with her, and he says she disappeared."

"Then we are going to find her," said Derek through gritted teeth. Anything else was impermissible.

"I agree." Kat squared her shoulders and looked at the ground between them for a moment, seeming halfway to whatever words she sought. "I wish I could accurately express how sorry I am that you all got dragged into this," she said at last, her voice soft and earnest.

Derek inhaled and let the breath out slowly. He knew Kat wasn't personally responsible for anything they had faced, and he couldn't let himself hold her accountable.

"Thank you," he said simply.

She turned and started for the cars, and then Lila emerged from around the corner. She approached Derek as Kat's footsteps faded.

"How much did you hear?"

"We'll find her, Derek. We will."

Lila closed the distance between them and wrapped him in her arms. For a moment, he stood stiff and distant, unwilling to let himself crumble. And then he embraced her, closing his eyes against the storm raging in his mind.

"This is my fault," he whispered. "I should've brought her with us. What was I thinking, leaving her to run the company when it's all over the news? There was no way Eddie and Mia weren't going to do something. I feel so stupid."

"You were protecting her," Lila said softly. "We had no idea what we were going to find. She's probably hiding somewhere until we come back and can figure out what to do about Mia."

Derek nodded slowly. He wanted to believe that Lila was right—that Desi was somewhere safe and choosing to remain off the radar. But he couldn't escape the gnawing feeling at the pit of his stomach that told him something far worse was happening.

"I…" Lila paused. She leaned back and looked away for a moment before meeting his eyes. "I didn't get the chance to comment on what you said while we were leaving West Point."

Derek's feet turned to lead. He wanted to sink into the ground and escape before she could shatter the small bit of hope he'd clung to that she could feel for him as he did for her.

"Yes?" he asked past the lump in his throat.

"I never thought you could feel that way about me," said Lila.

Her eyes shone with tears, and Derek fought down the urge to retract what he'd said if it was causing her pain.

"For years, I've wondered what it would be like to love someone. As long as I can remember, actually," she admitted, and in the shoddy light, he believed he saw her cheeks turn the slightest bit pink. "I remember what it was like to watch your parents and how they couldn't stop smiling when they were near each other."

The words sent a pang through Derek, but he said nothing.

"And I don't know when it happened, but somewhere along the line, I started to feel differently about you than I ever had about anyone else. I wanted to do absolutely everything to make you happy. And when I remembered that after… they messed with my memory, it killed me. It killed me to know what I'd done to you even more than it already had, because I remembered that I've loved you for longer

than I can remember. And that scares the hell out of me."
Lila let out a nervous laugh that Derek only half-registered
past the sudden screaming of his mind. Tears slipped from
her eyes as she spoke, and he wanted to reach out and wipe
them from her cheeks. "I don't know if I was supposed to
be built to love. I don't know if I'm allowed to feel this way
about anyone, least of all you. I've caused you so much
pain, and I know I don't deserve you." Her voice cracked,
and she paused. "But that doesn't change the fact that I love
you."

Derek stepped forward and laid his hands on Lila's
cheeks. All at once, he pulled her close and kissed her.

His heart thrummed so quickly he was certain it would
fly from his chest, but in that moment, he couldn't bring
himself to care.

"I love you," he whispered. He embraced her tightly,
afraid that if he let her go, he might lose her, too.

Chapter Fourteen

As he scanned his sister's apartment, Derek knew something was terribly wrong. The furniture was as he'd last seen it, all white-upholstered and pristine. But the telesense screen bore a crack down its center, and Desi's clothes lay scattered across her sheets and bedroom floor.

The others waited below in the cars, as they were certain stopping here was little more than a waste of time, but Lila was currently searching the kitchen for any hint as to where Desi could have gone, and Derek had left Ravenna searching the bedroom. He scoured the living room for anything else out of place, but he could find nothing.

Where the hell are you?

"Derek."

He looked up toward Lila's voice as she moved in a blur to his side. She held out her left hand and opened it to reveal shards of glass and porcelain.

"The trash can in the kitchen is full of this," she said. "Like someone smashed all her dishes and it got cleaned up quickly."

"Why would someone do that?" asked Derek. "If they'd gone to the trouble of getting in here, why would they go after the dishes and not Desi?"

"To scare her."

He turned to see Ravenna inspecting the crack in the telesense. After a second's pause, she spoke again.

"I doubt this was all they did. She probably fixed whatever else happened to pretend it didn't. Whoever broke in wouldn't have taken the time to clean up the glass."

"I also found this," said Lila.

She passed Derek a small piece of paper that had been crumpled into a ball. Slowly, he unfolded it. Though he knew realistically that a scrap of paper wasn't likely to harm him, this made him no more eager to see what may have driven his sister from her apartment.

You aren't fit to lead LDE. Resign before you no longer have the choice.

He swore under his breath and passed the note to Lila as Ravenna moved closer to inspect it, as well.

"We have to find her," he said, staring at the door to his sister's room. "I think someone else already has."

Eddie stared at her where she sat slumped on the grey-carpeted living room floor, her hands pressed to the bleeding wound over the right side of her ribs. He tried hard to summon her face to the front of his mind as it had been not long earlier—she'd smiled as she'd lain beside him, her dark blond hair falling lazily over the edge of his pillow and brushing his shoulder. The image held for only an instant before reality cracked through to reveal her here, her shirt soaked through with blood and her hands stained red.

"Desi?" he breathed.

Within the span of a heartbeat, he'd stood and started toward her, but before he could make it more than a step, Mia surged forward, placing herself between them.

"What the hell happened?" Eddie demanded, not bothering to hide the venom in his tone.

"Don't you realize she's a danger to us?" snapped Mia, her eyes narrowed and full of fire. "She knows about the Division. She knows they commissioned me, and she knows you went behind her brothers' backs to create me. She was going to the police, Eddie."

"You're insane," Desi muttered, shaking her head. "I wasn't going to tell anyone."

Eddie's stomach turned at the sight of the blood dappling her hair. He rounded on Mia, who took a step closer to him.

"Do you honestly believe her?" Mia pressed. "Do you really think she has any interest in telling you the truth, anymore?"

Eddie recalled the panic in which he'd turned Desi's attempt at retribution for Damian against her. When he'd realized they had no longer been alone in the warehouse, he'd taken the gun and held it to her temple, and though he never would've pulled the trigger, he couldn't expect her to know that.

He ignored Mia and brushed past her to Desi's side, crouching and laying a hand gently on her shoulder.

She wrenched away from his touch, hissing and clutching at her side as the movement upset her wound. It was all Eddie could do not to wince at her determination to escape him.

"What did she do to you?" he whispered.

"You mean besides causing the accident that killed my parents and helping you murder Damian?" Desi snarled. "Get away from me."

Eddie swallowed and stood.

"She's a liability," said Mia flatly.

"What do you want, Mia? What are you suggesting?" Eddie stared at her, studying the hard brown eyes he'd designed in a much simpler time. He'd been determined to help the Division bring the United States out of a military slump and save the lives of needlessly endangered soldiers, but Mia had never been his answer. From her first trial, she'd been nothing short of a plague.

"We need to protect ourselves," she said simply.

In a blur of auburn, she flew from the living room, returning seconds later with a sleek silver plasma gun in her hand.

"She knows too much, Eddie." Mia raised the gun and took aim at Desi's chest.

"Mia, put it down. Put it down now."

Eddie stepped toward her, his hands raised as his heart pounded sickeningly, feeling as though it were creeping its way up his throat. He spared a glance in Desi's direction to find her staring at the gun, her lips set firmly.

She won't beg Mia to stop. I think she'd welcome it, at this point.

The thought sickened Eddie. What had he done to her? To the woman he loved?

Mia tightened her grip on the gun, and Eddie was certain she would pull the trigger. He willed himself to move more quickly than he'd ever moved before, and in an instant, he stood between Mia and Desi, inches from the barrel of the gun.

Mia's eyes widened. As she watched him, Eddie understood everything he'd tried to block from his mind. He felt the ghost of Mia's fingers wrapped around his throat, and he remembered.

"You want to shut me down? For her?" she snapped.

Eddie pulled at her fingers, struggling to pry them from his neck, and he could only splutter and clutch at her as she lifted him just slightly and his feet lost their purchase on the warehouse floor. Her grip tightened.

"You—are—dangerous," Eddie choked.

"Whose fault is that?" Mia cried, her arm trembling. "I'm what you made me," she continued. "And you're supposed to love *me."*

Eddie attempted once more to speak, but he found himself unable to force words past the burning in his lungs. He surrendered, allowing his eyes to close.

He was only vaguely aware of the world around him as he was lowered carefully to the floor.

"Maybe the other you will," Mia whispered.

"I couldn't have moved that quickly," said Eddie, refusing to shift his focus from Mia's face.

"You're imagining things," said Mia with a tight shake of her head.

"No, I'm not."

Eddie reached for Mia's wrist and wrenched it to the side, and when she yielded with a sharp exhale, triumph washed over him along with a deluge of sadness.

"When did you replace me?" he hissed. "When I brought you out of storage to kill you?"

"You're delusional. And I don't want to hurt you, so let me go."

"What did you do to the other me? The—"

The next word died in Eddie's throat. He knew this was the truth his mind had been railing against, the secret that had come to him in flashes after he'd hit his head in the fight with Desi at the warehouse. He couldn't deny it any longer, now that he knew he was strong enough to restrain Mia, fast enough to outmaneuver her.

He remembered programming the copy of himself he and the Lawrence brothers had christened "E-2." He remembered the synthetic blood they'd poured into the copy's metallic veins and the extensive tests through which they'd replicated his own body, and he remembered when he'd decided to shut Mia down permanently. When she'd decided that perhaps she could persuade his copy to love her.

"What did you do with the real one?" he whispered.

Mia's eyes narrowed. "You are real, Eddie. Every bit of you. You're standing there with a very real choice, and you have the chance to make the right one, this time."

She wrenched her arm free and darted to the side, and as she retrained her weapon on Desi and squeezed the trigger, Eddie charged forward, throwing himself between them.

He felt the insurmountable burning of the plasma bolt as it sank into his chest, and he dropped to his knees. His eyes lost their focus on Mia, though he heard her scream, and after a moment, he abandoned his efforts to remain upright. He fell backward, half-processing the blood spilling from his chest and spreading warmth over him as it seeped outward along his shirt. He tasted liquid iron.

We did a damn good job designing it, didn't we?

He didn't want to spend more than an instant wondering if he could count himself among those creators.

He searched the room as well as he could without lifting his head, and he saw that Desi had managed to stand. She was staring at him, mouth open, visibly horrified.

"This is *your* fault!" Mia cried.

Eddie returned his focus to her as she raised the gun again. For the first time since her creation, he saw a tear sliding down her cheek.

"Put—it—down," said Eddie as he fought back the bloody cough he could feel rising in his lungs. "It won't—solve—anything."

Slowly, Mia lowered the gun. She crouched beside Eddie, laying the weapon down as she leaned over him, laid her head on his shoulder, and wept.

"I'm sorry. I didn't mean to—"

"I know."

Eddie wrapped his arm around Mia's back, hoping she understood the gesture as a comfort as he held her in place. He stretched the fingers of his free hand out over the soft grey carpet and wrapped them around the grip of the gun. He held her close as he pressed the barrel to her back and fired.

Mia convulsed once and collapsed heavily on top of Eddie. She was still.

He let out a long breath and shifted her off of him, and she landed on the floor with a thud, staring unblinkingly up at the ceiling.

He dropped the gun to the floor beside Mia and looked to Desi, who had taken a step toward him while he'd been looking elsewhere.

"She would have killed you," he said softly.

"I know."

At last, Eddie could hold back his coughs no longer. He spluttered and fought against the blood pooling in his throat, but he couldn't keep himself from coughing up some of it. Desi flinched as she watched him.

I don't want her to see me like this. So weak.

"I'll call an ambulance," said Desi.

"No. Please, just—just stay with me."

Slowly, she moved to his side and sat. Her blue eyes shone with unshed tears. He supposed she didn't want to allow herself to weep for him, and he couldn't blame her even an ounce.

"I'm sorry she hurt you," said Eddie. When she nodded stiffly, he continued. "And I'm... sorry for everything I've done to cause you pain."

At last, a tear broke free and slid down Desi's cheek.

"We could've..." She swallowed. "We could've been happy."

Eddie felt the sting of tears at the corners of his own eyes, and within a few seconds, Desi was blurry where she sat beside him.

"I'm sorry," he muttered. "So sorry. For all of it."

The real Eddie wouldn't have done this to you, he thought, but he couldn't allow himself to speak the words.

If she knew what he was, that he was just a flawed copy that had succumbed too easily to Mia's manipulations, she would leave him here to bleed to death alone.

"I don't expect you to forgive me," he said. "I could never ask that of you. Just know that... I never wanted to hurt you."

"Okay," she said with a small nod.

Eddie paused and studied her. One hand still held the wound Mia had given her, and he looked to the other.

"May I?" he asked. "Just once?"

She reached out and gave his hand the smallest of squeezes.

"Thank you," he said. "And I want you to have this." With his free hand, he reached into his pocket and withdrew his LDE keycard, passing it to her. She released his hand just long enough to set it beside her. "Go to the warehouse. You can use that to open the only locked door. You'll... understand."

The edges of his vision had begun to darken. He succumbed to another round of coughs, this one more ragged and violent than the last. When it subsided, he spoke once more.

"I know you don't feel it, Desi, but... I love you."

He felt her grip on his hand tighten, and for an instant, he imagined she'd said the words back to him. Then his limbs were too numb to feel. He struggled for breath as the darkness overtook his vision, and then he saw nothing.

Chapter Fifteen

"Rachel? Are you awake?"

Her eyes fluttered open at the sound of Andrew's voice, straining in the darkness and yet unable to make out anything. Her arms and legs were restrained; she fought to move them, but something at her wrists and ankles held her immobile. Her waist was trapped by something, as well, and she had no idea where she was.

"Yes."

"I hope you have a plan."

She laughed quietly. "I'm sure I'll think of one eventually," she said.

A sigh reverberated through the space, which sounded empty apart from the two of them.

"That's not what I'd hoped to hear," he said.

There was silence for several long seconds.

"I'm sorry, Andrew. I had to say something. They would have killed us if I hadn't."

"We're not actually going to lead them to Ravenna, are we?"

"Of course not. We're going to destroy them. I just… don't know how."

Light entered the room like the blast of an explosion. Rachel recoiled from it. She closed her eyes tightly and opened them again, waiting for them to adjust. When the room settled into coherence, Rachel surveyed it, taking in as much of her surroundings as she could process.

The light appeared to be emitted by a lamp hanging from the ceiling outside. It was bright for a single bulb, but it was not enough to cause such withdrawal under normal circumstances. Rachel assumed the effect was due to the time she had spent in dark oblivion.

The room was almost completely empty, filled with only old crates and mechanical parts that looked broken; even these were in short supply. Rachel's wrists and ankles were bound, held together by strips of metal twisted into alignment by her captors. A strip fastened around her waist kept her pressed to the wall, immobile. She remained fixed to the back corner of the room with the door set into the wall across from her. To her left, in the opposite corner, Andrew was similarly restrained. The sight of him in this horrid situation was as painful to Rachel as the metal vise.

In the doorway stood Hathor. The android was beautiful and intimidating at once, like a poisonous snake. She stepped into the room.

"All right." Hathor looked from Rachel to Andrew with an odd blend of interest and condescension. "Where is the assassin?"

"An answer for an answer. Where are we?" Rachel held the android's cool emerald gaze unflinchingly. She would not cower to the will of her captors, nor would she show fear.

Hathor laughed coldly. "You aren't in a position to make demands, Hartley. I won't play games with you. Tell me, or I kill him."

Hathor nodded to Andrew, whose eyes widened in terror. He apparently thought better of the reaction, because he forced it away, replacing the expression with one of indifference. Rachel knew he wanted to protect her from the guilt of making the decision as it should be made.

"Rachel, don't worry about me."

Hathor shot Andrew a withering look, and he said no more.

Rachel's heart pounded, and her thoughts swirled, fighting for a solution. She had no idea where the others were headed, but she knew that Ravenna was with Blue Team as well as several others. She hoped they had enough sense to stay together and stay safe, and, above all, to stay away from Washington. She knew it would be tempting to rendezvous with the Division personnel stationed in the nation's capital, but it was far too dangerous a chance to take. The androids would likely think to target the surviving Division installation, though hopefully those agents would know to make themselves scarce, given the circumstances and the attack on West Point.

"They're headed to Washington."

Hathor smirked. "See? That wasn't hard, was it?" She turned on her heel and started for the door.

"Wait!" called Rachel. "You have what you want! Now let us go!"

The android's laugh sent a chill through Rachel. "We have more plans for you than that." Without another word, Hathor left, dropping the door closed behind her.

"Why did you tell her they were going to Washington?"

Rachel sighed. "Because I hoped they wouldn't be stupid enough to do it, and I couldn't think of anything else that would keep the androids off their trail."

"But what if they do go there? Our people, I mean?"

"I don't know. I hope they don't. I don't know where they'll go—I don't even know where we are. But the androids want us all dead. If our people go to Washington, they're playing right into the plan. They won't stand a chance."

Desi stared blankly at the white curtain separating her from the hospital's other patients. She was feeling incredibly out of place, surrounded by worried doctors on the curtain's other side and her brother, who was still talking from the chair beside her bed even though she had stopped listening several minutes earlier.

For the duration of the trip to the emergency room, Desi had distanced herself from those around her, unable to speak as she and the paramedics had moved farther away from the man she had once loved. The sight of Eddie there, on the floor, had been too much to bear. After calling Derek—who had left twenty-two missed calls on the phone that had been silenced in her pocket since she'd left her apartment—to come to her aid, she had resigned herself to the corner, where she had become little more than a shell, no longer connected to her own mind or anything around her. She'd made half an attempt at explaining the situation to the paramedics and to Derek, and she had barely uttered a word since.

Eddie had been a liar. A murderer. A monster. So why did she ache with her every fiber, now that he was gone? Had she really been honest with herself when she had decided that she felt nothing more for him?

It's too late, Desi. It's too late.

He had killed her brother, but he had died for her.

"…got out as quickly as we could, when they attacked. We still haven't heard anything from Rachel or Andrew, and as soon as you're discharged, we need to get on the road. We can't take the chance on Osiris figuring out where we are."

When Derek stopped speaking, Desi blinked and returned her focus to his face at last. He'd already explained to her everything he knew of the Division and its secrets, including Mia's hand in the deaths of their parents, which she hadn't had enough strength left to admit she'd already known. Her ability to process the attack he'd described was nonexistent, at the moment, and she barely registered the sting left over from the lasers used to seal the wound just above her ribs. The doctors' orders to remain here and "take it easy" were nearly forgotten.

The keycard in the pocket of the pants she had draped over the chair beside Derek called to her, demanding her attention.

"Go to the warehouse. You can use that to open the only locked door."

Eddie's words echoed through her head, taunting her. What could have possibly been important enough to him to lead him to spend his last moments giving her the key? What was behind that door?

The need to know ate at Desi until she could stand it no longer.

She knew Derek would not approve of her investigating. Overprotective as he was, he would want to find out the truth for himself before allowing her to be put in another potentially dangerous situation, and he certainly wouldn't want her following a trail set by Eddie.

But the key had been meant for her, and she had to know.

"I'm sorry you went through all that," she said at last. "I… Derek, I need to use the restroom. I'll be back soon."

She sat up, and the pain in her ribs knocked the wind from her newly healed lungs. Derek moved to help her, but she slapped at his arm.

"I'm fine."

"No, you aren't."

Desi ignored him. She pushed herself to her feet and slipped on her shoes, closing the distance to the chair as quickly as she could.

"What are you looking for?" he questioned as she rifled through her pants pockets.

"My phone," she lied, slipping the keycard surreptitiously into the pocket of her gown before turning to face her brother. "It's not here. I think I left it with Lila and Ravenna."

"We can get it from them as soon as the doctors let them back here. And hopefully we'll be told soon how long they want you to stay."

She nodded vaguely and then threw her arms around Derek's neck, embracing him.

"Thank you. For coming to find me, I mean, and for bringing me here. I love you."

"I love you, too," he said, surprise evident in his voice.

"But I'm fine," she asserted. As she spoke, she gently grasped the key ring protruding from Derek's pocket and withdrew it. She paused for a moment, and when she was satisfied that he hadn't noticed, she took a step backward. "I'll be back."

She smiled and slipped through the curtain without another word, moving at a brisk walk until she had cleared the emergency room doors. Desi then broke into a run, nearly bumping into several people as she wove through the halls of the hospital. She flew out the front doors and into the dark parking lot, where she searched out Derek's car.

The road zoomed past her in a blur as she drove toward the place she had visited only once before, on one of the most traumatizing nights of her life. But that evening in July could not hold a candle to the one she found herself hurtling through now.

When she arrived, she found the concrete warehouse's perimeter covered with yellow police tape. Without hesitation, Desi slipped through the tape and into the building.

She stumbled through the darkness for what like hours before emerging, at last, into the immense room where she had once been held at gunpoint. Her breath shaky and uneven, Desi scanned the walls for a door.

There.

In the far corner, concealed almost entirely by the long metal staircase that rose to the observation deck, where the window was still shattered from the impact of a plasma bolt. Desi's body went cold at the sight, her pulse accelerating.

She jogged toward the door, ignoring her burning lungs, and paused for only the length of a heartbeat before producing the card.

"I came," she whispered as she scanned it through the panel set into the wall. "I don't know why, but it did."

The red light on the panel beside the door turned green, and the door slid open.

Lights flickered on to reveal what looked like a small laboratory, much like the one at LDE. Frowning, Desi stepped into the room, and the door sealed itself behind her. Apart from a single silver table to her left, the only item present was a chamber set into the back wall. It was covered by a glass dome, which was frosted over. She crossed the room silently to stand beside it. There was a control panel nearby, and at its center, she spotted a green button marked "Release."

I've come this far, Desi told herself. *Might as well go all in.*

She pressed the button.

Air hissed from either side of the dome, and slowly, the frost faded. Beyond the glass was a figure that became clearer with each passing second.

"No," Desi whispered.

Coughs sounded from the other side, mingling with deep breaths, gasps for air. Finally, the glass dome shifted to the right and slid back into the wall, revealing the figure within.

"Desdemona?"

The all-too-familiar grey eyes met hers, and she couldn't breathe. She couldn't think.

This isn't real.

Trembling, Desi began to back away from the sight before her. Had she not just witnessed Eddie's death? How could he be in front of her, struggling to catch his breath and working to steady himself as he took a shaky step away from the chamber?

She sank to the floor, staring blankly ahead, unable to focus. *This is impossible. This can't be happening. He's dead. He's dead.*

Slowly and unsteadily, Eddie lowered himself to the floor beside her, concern etched into each line of his face.

"This isn't real," Desi breathed.

"What do you mean? What happened to you? Are you hurt?"

Desi let out a clipped laugh at the absurdity of his questions. She glanced down at her hospital gown and then returned her focus to his face, to the lips she'd kissed more times than she wanted to admit to herself.

"I'm going insane."

"I don't think that's true," said Eddie, shaking his head. "Please, tell me what's wrong."

His eyes were filled to the brim with sincerity.

Either by some twist of fate he really has no idea, or he's a better liar than I thought. And that... would be saying something.

She took a deep breath, but the words she forced herself to say came out as scarcely a whisper.

"You're dead."

Chapter Sixteen

"I stand before you tonight because you have asked me to. I address you, as a nation, in response to requests from members of my Cabinet who believe that a certain pair of events has indicated a threat to our national security."

Ravenna sat in one of the hovering chrome chairs in front of the waiting room's large window, her chin resting on her folded hands. Her eyes were locked on the telesense on the opposite wall, where a silver-haired man stood at a podium addressing a mass of news cameras. A blue bar across the screen's bottom read "President Ethan McNaire."

Ravenna had never heard good things about McNaire, but since learning everything she had about the Division, she'd come to agree with him on at least one issue.

"I wish to assure you," McNaire continued, his expression grave, "that the attack on the home of Former President Isabella Hartley does not suggest a larger threat to our nation. The attack, which lead to the death of Miss Susan Rush, was an isolated incident. The Central Intelligence Agency has not connected the attack to any other covert or illegal activities that may pose a threat to the United States. Additionally, the fire that destroyed West Point was ruled an accident by the Federal Bureau of Investigation."

Ravenna nearly choked on the flat laugh that erupted from her lungs.

I think the people those psychotic androids murdered would take issue with your stupid cover-ups.

Footsteps thundered down the hallway adjoined to the waiting room, and Ravenna tore her gaze from the telesense to search out the source. Derek burst in, his sandy-blond hair wild and his eyes wide with alarm.

"She's gone," he said breathlessly.

"What do you mean, 'gone'?"

This came from Lila, who was seated at Ravenna's right.

"Desi disappeared. She took my car keys."

Silence followed. The only sound in the nearly deserted waiting room was the televised voice of McNaire.

"Former President Hartley has been placed under heavy protection. She is safe. Rest assured that you, too, are safe. Goodnight, America."

Ravenna's focus was ripped from Derek by the sound of a gunshot.

She whipped toward the screen, where McNaire fell instantly backward. Secret Service agents and converged on him, and he disappeared from view.

The camera panned dizzily to the side to halt on a dark-haired young reporter.

"This is Abdul Abaza for Channel Two News. The president has just been shot. I repeat," he called over the din that had erupted at the press conference, "President McNaire has just been shot!"

Frozen, Ravenna watched until she realized that the incoherent mass of shapes on the screen would not settle into a clear image. The frenzy had just begun.

She looked away and glanced from Derek to Lila to find that they were both staring in horror at the telesense. Despite the gravity of what she had just seen, Ravenna forced herself to return to the other potentially disastrous problem at hand.

"Derek, why would Desi take your keys?"

He blinked and returned his attention to her.

"I have no idea," he said. "She said she was going to the bathroom. I never should've let her leave the emergency room alone, not after everything that's happened today."

"No," said Lila, sliding to her feet and moving to Derek's side in a flash. "It's not your fault. Wherever she is, she obviously didn't want you to know she was going there. She would've found a way to do it regardless of what you said."

Derek nodded absently, his hands moving to his pockets. "I'll call her. Maybe she'll answer—" He halted.

"What's wrong?" Ravenna asked hollowly.

"My phone. I left it with Kat."

Ravenna closed her eyes and sighed, producing her own phone. At the sight of the screen, she frowned.

(6) Missed Calls.

Derek

Derek

Derek

Derek

Derek

Derek

Something was wrong. She tapped the screen and willed it to call Derek's phone. Before the first ring had finished, she heard Kat's voice.

"Are you still at the hospital?"

"Yes. I'm sorry, I didn't realize you call—"

"I need the four of you to get back here as soon as possible. We have a problem."

Ravenna's frown deepened as she locked eyes with Derek.

"What kind of problem?" she asked.

"The body we found does not belong to Edward Dodson."

"What do you mean, *I'm dead?*"

He was just as she remembered him. The same dark hair, the same grey eyes, the same concerned expression she'd known for more than half her life.

Eddie was anything but dead.

He was utterly unharmed, despite the fact that hours earlier, Desi had held his hand as his last breath had left his body.

How, then, was he sitting beside her now with no idea what she was talking about?

"You were shot in the chest right in front of me," she breathed. "You bled to death."

She was numb. Gone were the feelings of trepidation, fear, and blatant curiosity that had filled her only moments before as she had approached the chamber. The crushing sense of loss that had turned her feet to lead had dissolved, replaced by a complete dissociation with reality and understanding.

Eddie spoke calmly, contrary to how Desi believed he should be reacting.

"Who shot me, Desdemona?"

Desdemona.   Her full name. He hadn't called her this—at least not willingly and not without a fair bit of badgering—since the beginning of their ill-fated relationship at the end of July. The sound of the name was nearly as strange to her as warmth she felt from his proximity.

"Mia," she said.

Eddie's jaw clenched almost imperceptibly. "Mia?"

"Enough." Frustration penetrated Desi's formerly flat tone. "Enough with the games. Mia, the android you created for the Division. The one responsible for God knows how many deaths."

Eddie flinched, but he quickly regained his composure and the smoothness of his features. "How do you know her?" he asked cautiously.

"Derek explained everything I didn't hear straight from her or you."

He frowned. "Derek? Isn't he away on business?"

It was Desi's turn to frown. "Business?" She shook her head. "He hasn't taken a business trip since—" She froze, her eyes wide.

He's completely serious. Almost like he... doesn't know. But of course he does. Doesn't he?

"What day do you think it is?" she asked quietly.

He answered without a second's hesitation. "It's July twenty-fourth."

The words knocked the breath from Desi's lungs. If Eddie thought it was still the day before the murder...

"Eddie, where is Damian?"

Again, he gave no pause. He did, however, appear thoroughly confused by her questions, and he raised a brow.

"He's out of town, too. He'll be home tomorrow. We talked about this when I picked you up from the police station. Did—" His expression grew suddenly panicked as he surveyed her hospital gown. "Did you get into an accident? What happened to you?"

Desi stared at him. She took in the earnestness of his concern, the fear in his eyes at the thought of harm coming to her.

This was not the same man who had held her at gunpoint.

"Damian won't be home tomorrow," she said gently, though each word still felt like the blow of a hammer against her chest. "My brother… he's dead."

Eddie watched her blankly, uncomprehending. "What?"

Her mind scrambled for options, for ways to spin her brother's fate that didn't make the situation at hand exponentially worse. She could find none.

"You killed him," she said.

Eddie's face fell, his expression overtaken by revulsion. "No. I didn't. You know I could never do something like--"

"You reprogrammed Lila to shoot him. You wiped her memory and showed Derek a security video that made him think she was completely responsible." The words flowed forth in a torrent, unstoppable now that they had begun. "I hired Ravenna to find Lila, but Derek protected her while you and I—" Desi halted, her mind filled with the taste of his lips and the butterflies that had erupted through her stomach at his touch. "Do you expect me to believe that you don't remember? Any of this—the last few weeks? It's not July twenty-fourth, Eddie, it's…" She glanced at the clock on the wall, which told her that it was not yet midnight. "August tenth."

He let out a heavy sigh. "The last thing I remember is being in this room. Since you apparently already know everything there is to know about Mia…"

She nodded, and he paused, holding her gaze for a moment too long. She supposed he was searching her for whether she knew what Mia had done to her parents. Her lips pressed into a tight line.

"…it won't hurt to tell you that I'd pulled her out of storage. I was going to deactivate her. After the way things were between you and me during that car ride when you wouldn't talk to me about what's happened between us, I—I couldn't stand it. I know I don't deserve you, Desdemona. Not after what I've done. I created her to help people, and all she's ever done is kill. I… I wanted to make up for some small fraction of it. I thought the first step was shutting her down."

Desi blinked. Eddie had said something similar when he'd put himself between her and Mia, but she'd been too consumed by fear and the loss of blood to pay it much attention.

Eddie stared at the floor for a long moment, and slowly, a look of horror dawned over his face.

"She started to strangle me," he said. "She must've knocked me out. The last thing I remember was her saying that I was supposed to love her. And that maybe—" He looked to the chamber from which he'd emerged, and then he closed his eyes. "Maybe the other me would."

"What the hell does that mean?" Desi pressed. She leaned back and wrapped her arms around her knees, certain that the cold chill that had swept over her was due to more than just her hospital gown.

"Maybe it was me," said Eddie softly as he returned his focus to her face. The pain in his eyes suggested his world had been snapped in two. "Maybe I did all those terrible things. But it wasn't the real me."

Kat drove at a speed far past the legal limit as she wove through the labyrinthine streets of Manhattan, searching for the hospital where the others waited for her. Derek's cell phone rested in the cup holder, and her own was pressed to her ear.

"What do you mean, there was nothing we could do?" she demanded. "We're supposed to be prepared for things like this, damn it!"

"I know. Agent Seward, I would appreciate it if you would calm down. I'm just the messenger." The voice on the other end of the phone belonged to John Beck, the head of the Division's branch in the nation's capital. "With Rachel gone, I didn't know who else to call."

Kat's knuckles tightened on the steering wheel, and she took a deep breath. She did not need to be reminded that Rachel was missing in action along with Andrew. Since her call with McNaire, Kat and the members of her team had received notifications from several of their field agents confirming their safety, but Rachel and Andrew still had not resurfaced.

"My cousin will find us when she's ready," Kat told John. Her words alluded to a confidence that she certainly did not feel. In truth, she was petrified. What if something had gone horribly wrong when the two had left to find Isabella? What if they were hurt?

What if they were dead?

Kat shook these thoughts away. Pessimism would do nothing to help her now.

"In the meantime," she said, "explain to me exactly what happened."

Beck sighed. "The president was giving a speech to calm the fears that the attack at your aunt's home was connected to something bigger. He told the nation it was safe. Then they shot him."

"Does 'they' mean what I think it does?"

"We have no idea. We helped the FBI seal off the area and perform a search, after we got McNaire out. We found absolutely nothing that could connect the attempt with anyone, human or android."

Kat glared as lights whipped past her outside the car, unsure how to work her frustration into a response.

"Between you and me," said Beck, dropping his voice to near inaudibility, "I wouldn't doubt that it was the 'them' we're looking for. They attacked West Point. All bets are off."

"I was afraid you'd say that." Distracted, Kat nearly missed her turn. She maneuvered the car rather sharply into the hospital's parking lot, slammed on the brakes, and watched a group of three dark shapes move through the darkness toward her. "I take it Cameron has been sworn in."

"He's taking the Oath as we speak."

"All right. Keep me posted, John."

"Of course."

She hung up the phone as Derek opened the passenger side door and slid into the car. Both back doors were opened, and Lila and Ravenna entered. Kat glanced into the rearview mirror to see that Charlie had managed to keep pace with her in the car borrowed from one of their contacts and was awaiting their next move. Casey was with Charlie, and Clarisse still sat at the back of the SUV Kat had driven away from West Point. Kat had known that when they recovered Desdemona, the SUV wouldn't hold everyone, if she planned to bring her entire team.

She had no idea how she was going to keep this many people safe when she hadn't been able to protect her cousin.

"I don't even know where to start with how wrong this is," Kat told Derek as she made a circle through the lot and pulled back onto the road, Charlie in tow.

He sighed. "Don't bother."

"So your sister stole your car and disappeared."

"Don't," said Derek again, more forcefully this time. "I don't need to hear it. I never thought I'd be grateful for something like a tracking device being put on my car."

Kat smirked.

"But why did you do it?"

"I didn't. Not personally, anyway. When you came to the base, Rachel wasn't sure if you could be trusted yet. She was afraid you might try to leave before we had a chance to find out what you knew. Don't look so offended," she told Ravenna, whose expression, visible in the mirror, was indignant. "We could've planted them on the three of you instead."

"Where are we going?" Derek asked.

Kat handed him a small, square monitor. "Why don't you tell us?"

There was a pause. "Naturally," Derek said at last. "The warehouse on Fifth Street."

As Kat watched in the rearview mirror, Lila groaned from the backseat. Ravenna dropped her head into her hand and closed her eyes. Nothing more was said as Derek passed the monitor back to Kat and she followed its directions to the warehouse. She turned on the radio to keep her thoughts away from what might have happened to her cousin and what was to happen to all of them, with not even the president safe from the androids the Division had unleashed upon the world.

When the blinking light on the monitor's screen was directly on top of the one representing Kat's car, she switched the device off and placed it in the glove box in front of Derek. She pulled the car onto the gravel outside the warehouse and turned off the engine, slipping the keys into her pocket.

Kat opened the door and stepped outside, the others filing out after her. Her agents approached from the other car.

"There's no point in splitting up," she told the group at large. "I don't imagine we're in any danger."

Casey laughed humorlessly. "How do you know?"

"My sister isn't a threat," hissed Derek. "Come on."

He turned away and moved toward the dark, police-tape-covered building, his anger evident even in the darkness. Kat shot Casey a reproving look and followed Lila, who had started after Derek. The LDE co-president's familiarity with the warehouse was made clear as he moved through the dim building without even a moment's pause or a falter in his steps. He managed to lead them into an immense room filled with innumerable metal platforms and stacks of crates. The last few in the procession had not yet entered the room when Derek came to an abrupt halt, his focus fixed on a door nearly obscured by a long staircase.

"I have a bad feeling about this."

"What?" Lila asked, taking his arm. "What's wrong?"

He slowly shook his head and started forward again. Kat's eyes narrowed as she followed, unease forming in the pit of her stomach. She motioned for the others to come along, though she didn't turn to see whether they looked as confused as she felt.

When they had reached the door, Derek produced a keycard and scanned it through the panel set into the wall. Kat watched his shoulders rise and fall with a deep breath as the door slid open, her fingertips brushing the gun at her side on reflex.

Lila gasped, her hands flying to her mouth. Derek faltered and caught himself by leaning on the doorway. As her heart pounded obnoxiously in her ears, Kat slid to the side to see into the room beyond past the stunned pair standing in front of her.

This isn't possible.

Near the center of the room, leaning against what resembled an operating table, sat Desdemona Lawrence and a man who could be none other than Edward Dodson.

"How the hell—?"

"Derek?" asked the seated man, looking from one face to the next.

"I always knew it was a bad idea," said Derek, watching his former business partner with his lips twisted in disdain.

"What?" asked Lila. "What's going on?"

"E-2."

Chapter Seventeen

Eddie was numb. He couldn't stretch his mind enough to wrap it around everything Desi had told him, and as he stared at the group in the doorway, he could only blink and hold his silence. Why was Derek here? And Lila? And who was the red-haired woman standing behind them? The things Desi had told him were a foreign language; they were at once alien and plausible.

He knew what must have happened. When he'd realized that the cryogenic chamber was empty and that he had been its occupant until she had freed him, the flashes of himself with Mia in this room had exploded through his mind, unbidden and unwelcome.

Mia had betrayed him. And, by the sound of what he had missed, she had done much worse than that.

Lila was frowning deeply, her perfect face made no less so by the expression. "What is E-2?" she asked.

Derek sighed. He ignored the question and instead addressed Eddie.

"Which one are you?"

"The real one," Eddie answered, finding his voice at last. "Though I suppose I would say the same if I weren't."

"They said the body they found wasn't yours." Derek's voice was hollow, his expression guarded. Eddie had no idea whether the news that he wasn't dead had been welcome to his best friend, and the thought dizzied him. "How did it happen?"

"Mia traded me for him."

"Will someone please explain what the hell is going on here?" asked the redhead standing beside Derek and Lila.

"There's no reason for everyone to stay standing," said Derek flatly, an edge of dark humor to his voice. Eddie had never seen him this cold. "It's a long story." Derek stepped into the room, followed by Lila. After them entered the redhead, along with two more women dressed in black. At the rear of the group were two whom Eddie recognized: Clarisse Mitchell and Ravenna, who Eddie had learned was seeing Damian on the last day he recalled. The day he'd come here to shut down Mia. The newcomers made themselves comfortable, taking seats on the table or in chairs or leaning against the wall.

Eddie addressed Derek, feeling suddenly overwhelmed and crowded. "Who are all these people?"

"You wouldn't recognize us," said the redhead. "You didn't come to West Point with Mia for her second trial. I'm Kat Seward, and we're all from the Division."

Eddie nodded slowly, glancing to Desi for some semblance of comfort in this room full of strangers. She would not look at him.

He tore his eyes from her and looked instead to Kat. "Why are you here?"

"I'd like to ask you the same question. Until a few minutes ago, we were convinced that you were dead."

Eddie's stomach twisted.

"Until, that is," Kat went on, "my team prepared to move your body and Mia's out of the house where you shot each other, and we realized that there was something off about your wound. Human tissue should have made much more of a mess after taking plasma to the chest. The shot was too clean. Apart from the blood, that is. Or whatever was substituted for it. The closer we looked, the less human we realized the body was."

"You're saying," interjected Ravenna from where she stood, glaring and tense, along the wall, "that the Eddie that Mia killed…?"

"Was an android," said Kat simply.

"I hoped to never have to talk about this again,"said Derek. His eyes took on a distant quality as a scowl settled onto his face. "After my parents died, Damian, Eddie, and I became interested in the idea of preserving human memories and knowledge after death. More than interested. Fixated. Obsessed. We wanted to find a way to avoid losing someone completely, even though they wouldn't technically be them."

"And what did we do for a living?" asked Eddie, taking over the explanation in an effort to make it easier on Derek. *I owe him so much more. So much that I'll never be able to repay it.* "We designed androids. What better way could there be to keep someone alive than in a form far less susceptible to harm than a human? It would be safer. More practical."

"Perfect."

Eddie glanced at Clarisse, who had spoken. Their eyes met, and he knew that she understood. The Division had sought perfection, and so its leaders had turned to androids. *For all the good it did them*, he thought.

"Yes. We discovered a way to connect to the human brain and, in a sense, upload and download information. Memories, feelings, thoughts, all transferable. The process was… morally objectionable, to say the least."

"And potentially dangerous," added Derek.

Eddie nodded. "I volunteered to be the test subject."

"Why?" The voice came from beside Eddie, and he turned to see that Desi was watching him, searching him. "Why would you volunteer for something like that?"

"I…" He faltered. *What do I say? 'I felt guilty for inadvertently causing the deaths of your parents, and I wanted to make it up to your family?' She would never understand. She would never forgive me. I can't tell her that.* "I wanted to help in any way I could," he said instead. "The three of us created another android, one modeled exactly in my image. We named him 'Edward-2.' 'E-2.' He retained my every memory, my every thought. My every feeling." He paused, his eyes lingering on Desi for an instant before returning to the rest of the group. This was not the time. "He was an incredible copy. He did, however, have one major flaw. He lacked my inhibitions. In our tests, we learned that, while we thought in remarkably similar ways on the majority of matters, his morality was… somewhat clouded. This was something we were never fully able to explain."

"The Division had the same problem," said Clarisse, who had paled considerably. "Which is why we came to you."

"I know." Eddie swallowed, attempting to focus on the present instead of the innumerable regrets of the past flooding his mind. "We succeeded, with Lila and those androids based on her. But the process was so different in creating E-2 that we had to start from scratch. We were never able to recreate that aspect of humanity perfectly, with him."

"So what did you do with him?" asked Desi. "After he was finished?"

Her brother answered. "We decided not to tell anyone until the process was perfected. We kept E-2 here, in the cryogenic chamber, deactivated and in suspended animation. We planned to return to the project, but time got away from us."

The blond Division agent cleared her throat. "How does a frozen android figure into this mess?"

Eddie sighed. "The last thing I remember was talking to Mia, here in this room. It was July twenty-fourth. E-2 was still here, then. We talked about…" He trailed off. In present company, it was probably best to avoid going into specifics regarding his and Mia's topic of conversation. He hesitated for only a beat. "…her Division trial, and I wanted to shut her down, and then she attacked me. She choked me until I blacked out, and then she…" He took a deep breath. "She must have switched me with him. You said that she and I shot each other." Eddie looked from Kat to Desi and back again. "I take it that means they're…"

"Both dead," Kat finished for him. "Yes."

Despair washed over Eddie. Two of his creations, destroyed. He had been powerless to save them. With the horrid things Mia was responsible for, he knew he had no reason to mourn her. Regardless, he had cared for her, though the knowledge that she had brought about Damian's death lessened the blow.

"We need to regroup with the Knights and get out of New York." Kat turned to Derek. "We'll stop by the hospital and get your sister officially discharged. I trust she won't make any more misguided attempts to go out on her own. That would be incredibly reckless." She shot Desi a stern look and left the room, followed by the two women Eddie didn't know.

Desi sighed. "I had to know what was here. Eddie—E-2, whatever—gave me the keycard, and I had to know. Here." She slipped the card from the pocket of her hospital gown and handed it to Eddie. She then stood and opened her mouth as though she wanted to say more, but instead, she gave her head a small shake. She silently followed the Division women out of the room.

Clarisse moved to Eddie's side and helped him to his feet. "These aren't the circumstances I'd hoped would bring us together again," she said solemnly.

"That makes two of us. I hope Mia didn't cause too much damage."

Clarisse laughed sadly, shaking her head. "You have no idea."

Without another word, she departed. Ravenna refused to so much as look in Eddie's direction. She folded her arms across her chest and stormed out after her aunt. He couldn't say he blamed her for her behavior. If E-2 could be blamed for Damian's death, then it might as well have been Eddie who had pulled the trigger.

He was left, now, with Derek and Lila.

"Whatever E-2 has done in my place, I want you to know that I would do anything to undo it. If there's some way that I can even begin to fix what's happened—"

"I know." Derek inhaled deeply. "They do, too." He indicated the doorway through which the others had disappeared. "It's just going to take a while for them to come to terms with the idea that you're innocent. And that's not to mention the rest of the world. Or my sister."

"Derek, what happened between her and E-2?"

"He broke her heart. That's something I don't want to see happen again."

Even after Derek and Lila had left the lab, the warning in those last words hung in the air. So he knew, then. He had realized that for E-2 to fall in love with Desi, Eddie had to feel the same way. Derek knew, at last, what Eddie had kept from him for years.

Eddie would not make the same mistake his double had made. He kept this thought at the forefront of his mind as he turned off the lights and walked out of the lab for what he now knew was the first time in over two weeks.

E-2 had apparently shared his feelings with Desi. Eddie intended to do the same. He, however, would rather die than hurt her.

But could she ever forgive him for what he had already done?

Kat scanned the living room where the bodies had been. Blood stained the grey carpet, but neither Mia nor E-2 was anywhere to be found.

"How the hell did this happen?" she demanded.

Lex and Abigail sat on the sofa, the former cradling an arm that looked broken even at Kat's distance and the latter favoring her injured ankle as she sat.

"For starters," said Abigail, "we should've determined what this place was before leaving anyone here."

"And what is it?" Kat didn't entirely manage to keep the snap from her tone, which she regretted as soon as she'd spoken, but she hadn't anticipated the Knights to be ambushed and lose the bodies they'd been tasked with monitoring.

"Hathor's house," said Lex flatly.

Kat's eyes widened. "How do you know?"

"First of all," Lex went on, "there are pictures of her and Horus in what has to be their bedroom. Second, Bastet and Anubis kicked the shit out of us. I'm pretty sure they only left us alive so we could warn you."

"They said there's nowhere we can go that they won't find us," said Abigail, her tight-lipped expression grave.

Kat sighed heavily. "So what do we do? Considering that it's..." She glanced down at the watch she wore and blinked. "...almost two in the morning, I'd say that attempting to drive too far now might not be a great idea. We're all dead tired as it is. We could stay somewhere, at least until it's light outside. We can't lose too much time, but I don't want to risk anyone getting into an accident. Again."

"We're going to Washington, right?"

Kat turned for the doorway to find Ravenna surveying the room. Kat had told everyone apart from Charlie and Casey to remain in the cars, and they were searching the house for evidence. She supposed she shouldn't be surprised that Ravenna had disobeyed.

"Yes, we are."

"We could stay with my parents, then. On the way."

"I don't want to put them in danger," said Kat.

"We won't be. The androids have no reason to suspect that we would go there. I haven't been home in…" She paused, thinking. "Probably fourteen years."

Lex frowned. "Are you sure we wouldn't be imposing?"

Ravenna shook her head. "I need to speak to them anyway. I guess while we're running for our lives is as good a time as any."

Abigail shrugged. "She has a point."

"It's settled, then." Kat nodded in appreciation to Ravenna. "Thank you. We'll let you lead the way, if you don't mind."

"I'll tell Derek to give me the keys," said Ravenna. She left the room.

"Everything about this feels wrong," said Kat quietly.

"That's because it is," said Abigail. "We were never supposed to have to fight them."

"We should've seen it coming." Kat shook her head and moved for the door. "Let's go."

Osiris reclined against the wall, waiting. The voices beyond the door at his side crescendoed and then ceased, followed by the approach of footsteps. Hathor appeared beside him as the door closed.

"Washington. I try to find out more every time I go in, but they won't say anything else. I could start breaking bones, if you like."

He smirked. "It's enough for now. They'll talk eventually."

She nodded, appearing thoroughly unmoved by his approval. "Have the others returned?"

"Yes."

The two looked up simultaneously at the melodic voice that echoed through the shadows of the tunnel. One of the lights hanging above cast its glow on Isis, who walked toward them from across the metal tracks lining the ground.

"The plan went perfectly," she said as she reached Osiris's side and wrapped her arms around his neck, amusement in her green eyes. "Not that I had any doubt. Horus is on the ground level," she added in curt aside to Hathor. "He's looking for you."

The scarlet-haired android did not acknowledge her blond companion verbally, but she disappeared into the dark edges of the tunnel. After a few moments, the sound of her footsteps had faded entirely.

"According to Hartley," said Osiris, "the humans are headed to Washington."

Isis gave a short laugh. "It's like they want us to win." She traced the long, jagged scar that ran from his left temple to his jaw with her thumb.

"And we will." At last, he felt his tension beginning to fade, and he laid a hand on the small of her back. Everything was falling into place more easily than he had dared to dream. "Anubis and Bastet should be arriving anytime with Mia."

A cynical chuckle resounded through the space. "In a manner of speaking."

Osiris removed his gaze from Isis to see the dual forms of their allies emerging from a passage a short distance down the tunnel. Each carried a large bundle.

"Things didn't go as expected," said Bastet, shaking her head.

Osiris tensed. "In what way?" He couldn't afford unnecessary complications when their plans were so near to fruition.

As one, Bastet and Anubis dropped their burdens to the stone ground in front of Isis and Osiris. Each object was wrapped in what looked like a blanket, and each covering bore scattered spots of dark red. A foreign feeling bubbled within Osiris, setting his limbs tingling uncomfortably. He was uncertain what to call it, but he imagined he was experiencing something similar to terror. He knelt beside the nearest of the objects and moved a careful hand to the shroud. With a well-concealed deep breath, he pulled it away to reveal what was within.

She was pale and frightening, her open eyes staring unblinkingly upward, and the familiar face caused him to recoil. He who had never known fear was faced with it in glaring finality upon realizing that this dead figure was none other than Mia. His ally—the visionary responsible for the plan that would bring undying glory to the androids at last, and the one who would now never experience that future.

"How?" Osiris asked shortly.

"We don't know," answered Anubis, "but we figure it had something to do with him." In one fluid movement, he pulled back the second blanket, revealing the famous face of robotics pioneer Eddie Dodson. Osiris merely blinked in surprise.

"Dodson's dead?" asked Isis, stunned.

"Looks can be deceiving." Bastet crouched beside the bodies and pulled the bloodstained blanket farther down to reveal a chest wound. On closer inspection, apart from on the surface, no tissue was visible. Instead, Osiris's gaze fell on circuits and metal.

"She went through with it," he muttered.

Isis frowned. "With what?"

"Mia talked with me about the copy they made of Dodson. She said he might be more sympathetic to our cause than the original, but she never said more about it."

He removed his gaze from the dead and looked to the sign made visible by the dim light above them. It read "Subway Network, Washington, District of Columbia."

"We have work to do," he said.

Chapter Eighteen

The car moved silently to a halt. Ravenna took a deep breath to steel herself to what was to come, and she opened the door.

"Wait here," she instructed Derek and Lila, who nodded. They didn't object, for which Ravenna was thankful. This was something she needed to do on her own.

She slid out onto the gravel of the driveway. Gently, she closed the door and turned away from the safety of the car and into the blackness broken only by lamps extending to her left and right. They lit the path from the enormous old house to various locations on its grounds, including stables and a pond that was known to freeze rapidly in winter. Pulling her thoughts away from that body of water—which must surely be only water midway through August, anyway—Ravenna moved from the driveway to the asphalt path.

She slipped through the shadows of the ancient property toward the house she had so long avoided and all the memories it kept locked inside. Every day since her departure, she had revisited this place in her mind, though never physically in that span. To do so would have been too painful.

It's because of what happened here that I'm not who I was. That I became a killer. That I lost my humanity.

At last, she reached the stone steps that led to the front doors and began to climb. A glance over her shoulder told her that the others had all remained in their vehicles. Ten pairs of eyes watched her, waiting to see if she would go through with it.

"I've come this far," she told herself quietly but evenly aloud. "I'm not going back, now."

She raised her fist, trembling slightly as it was, and knocked on one of the large oak doors.

Not a sound followed apart from the chirping of the crickets and cicadas in the trees. Ravenna remained perfectly still and waited. When after several moments nothing had happened, she knocked again—this time louder, more insistently. For at least thirty seconds, she knocked, determined to have them hear her, to acknowledge her.

Finally, she heard soft footsteps from within that grew rapidly closer and were followed by the clicking of locks. The doorknob and Ravenna's stomach twisted, and the door was pulled open.

A tan woman with long black hair stood on the threshold. She wore a blue nightgown, and her feet were bare. Her brown eyes were only half-open, and she stifled a yawn. A long moment passed before her gaze fell on Ravenna. Then suddenly, her tired eyes widened, and she stumbled, clutching the doorframe for support.

A whisper broke the silence. "Ravenna?"

The younger woman swallowed. "Hi, Mom."

Her mother struggled for words. In lieu of speaking, she pulled Ravenna into her arms. Tears stung Ravenna's eyes as she embraced her mother, who was shorter than her, now.

"I'm sorry," she said. "I'm sorry I didn't come home. I… I couldn't."

"You can always come home," said Leah Mitchell, who did not release her daughter. "No matter what, we love you."

The tears broke free, streaming down Ravenna's cheeks and onto her mother's shoulder. She had waited so long to say the words that they seemed to take a part of her with them as they left her lips. "I love you, too."

Several seconds passed in contented silence, which was broken eventually by a timid voice from behind Ravenna.

"Leah, I owe you an explanation. And an apology."

Leah and her daughter released one another and turned simultaneously to face the newcomer. Ravenna frowned slightly. She had not seen or heard her aunt following her to the door. Clarisse stood a few feet behind Ravenna, her head hung slightly, allowing her dark hair to fall forward and cast further shadows across her penitent face. Her niece watched through narrowed eyes, wary of the elder woman's apologies.

"Clarisse?" Leah folded her arms across her chest as she studied her sister-in-law. "I don't understand." She looked from Clarisse to Ravenna and back again. "You've both been gone for so long. Why now?"

Ravenna sighed. Now that she had led the others here, she regretted that decision greatly. They would have to leave as soon as possible; they were in too much danger to stay long without putting the Mitchells at risk. Once again, Ravenna would have to say goodbye to her parents without knowing when or if she would see them again. She would have to lie. After all, how could she explain the threat that encroached on her mind from every angle without giving away secrets that weren't legally hers to pass on? How was she to ask her mother and father to take in her friends without knowing the truth? And why should her parents help her, after everything she had done? She didn't deserve it. But now she had given the others her word that she would try, and she had no other option.

"Mom, we need your help."

Leah frowned. "What could I help you with?" She blinked, shaking her head in what looked like bemusement. "I love you both, but I can't imagine what use I could be to you, after all this time."

Ravenna swallowed the lump rising in her throat. Her heart ached, and she wished with all of her being that she could erase the pain she had left her parents to endure for the last fourteen years.

"We've brought some friends with us," she told her mother. "Can we stay here tonight?"

Without hesitation, Leah nodded. "Of course you can. If it means I can have my family together again for one night, you can bring as many friends as you want."

A short laugh escaped Ravenna's lips. "You'll wish you hadn't said that. But thank you." She smiled, and the gesture seemed to free something within her. Her lungs felt a bit less constricted, and an invisible weight disappeared from her chest.

Clarisse was also smiling. This must have been un-intentional, for in an instant, her expression had returned to neutrality. "I'll go tell the others."

She turned away and started down the stone steps.

"Clarisse."

The woman addressed paused, turning her head toward Leah, who had spoken.

"Don't forget that explanation you owe me."

This time, Clarisse didn't attempt to hide her smile as she disappeared down the steps. Ravenna and her mother stood in a rather comfortable silence. Breathing in deeply, Ravenna looked out across the lawn, willing this place to feel like home. In her childhood, it had belonged to her grandparents. She had kept tabs on her family from afar after she'd left home, using her friends in assassins' guilds in New York to search out information. She'd learned that her grandmother had fallen ill a few years after her departure and that her parents had moved in to help her grandfather care for her. As far as Ravenna knew, her grandparents, now in their early nineties, were still living in the house. They were most likely asleep, given the time. Ravenna wondered if it would be best if she left before they knew she had returned home.

"Am I dreaming?"

Ravenna turned toward the voice, and the tears returned to her eyes at the sight of her father. He was Clarisse's double, down to the grey flecking his hair.

"She's really here, Aiden," said Leah.

Ravenna's father pulled her into his arms silently. He asked for no answers and no reasons, and she did not try to speak.

Feet clattered loudly up the stone steps, and Clarisse reappeared, followed by Derek, Lila, Desi, Eddie, and the Division members. Aiden released Ravenna, moving to stand between her and his wife as he watched the newcomers with confusion.

Clarisse faltered when her eyes met those of her brother. Everything she wanted to say to him appeared to fight for dominance, resulting in her inability to say anything. She took a step forward, hesitated, and then embraced him. Eventually, she found her voice.

"I'm sorry, Aiden. You deserved the truth, and it was the one thing I couldn't afford to give you. I want to make things right with you and Leah."

"Don't apologize," said Aiden. "It was your job."

"If you'll all come with me," said Leah to the others, "I'll show you to the guest rooms. We have several, and most have more than one bed. They're right this way."

She led them through the foyer. Derek nodded to Ravenna in appreciation as he passed, and the group disappeared up the stairs. Clarisse followed them after a few moments, and Ravenna and Aiden were left alone.

"Dad, there's something I need to tell you."

He watched her with understanding in his hazel eyes. "What is it, Rae?"

"You're going to be a grandfather."

Eddie sighed into the darkness. He found it impossible to sleep, given the stress of all that he had learned in only a few short hours.

I am responsible for the death of my best friend. My creation replaced me with my copy and ran amuck through New York, causing irreparable damage. And now no one trusts me. Can I blame them, really?

He closed his eyes and shook his head against the pillow. In Derek's place, Eddie knew that he would do no differently. Keeping a government agent in the same guest room Eddie occupied in the Mitchells' home wasn't all that unreasonable, under the circumstances.

Pausing, Eddie listened. Lex breathed rhythmically from the bed nearest the door, presumably asleep. The steady ticking of a clock was the only other sound in the room. Eddie had no idea how long he had been lying here or what time it was, but he truly had no desire to know. He was exhausted, though he felt that having slept for the last several weeks precluded the notion of returning to oblivion. Everything had become so strange around him. What was to say that if he returned to sleep, he would wake up here? What if this was all a dream, and he was still frozen in the lab, with his subconscious mind only now aware of his situation?

Stop it, he ordered himself. *Of course you're awake. You've just been betrayed, and that has left you skeptical of absolutely everything.* He pressed his palms to his eyes. *Derek and Damian were right. You should never have created Mia.*

He could take no more of this. Silently, he slid from beneath the covers and stepped onto the carpet. He crept across the room, taking care not to wake Lex as he passed by the other bed on his way to the door. Eddie twisted the doorknob, which clicked, and he glanced nervously over his shoulder to find that Lex had not moved. Relieved, Eddie opened the door, closing it behind him after he stepped into the hall.

Had he not known better, he would have thought the house deserted. It was incredibly quiet and still. Not another soul occupied the hall he now moved through like a ghost. At least he thought so, until she spoke.

"I guess I'm not the only one who can't sleep."

His heart skipped a beat, and his stomach fluttered as though he had missed a step on a staircase. Eddie turned to face her, wondering how she could have been quiet enough to enter the corridor without his notice. She stood a few rooms back, leaning against the doorframe and watching him closely. In her blue eyes, he saw a mixture of resignation and curiosity. She wore a white nightgown he knew must've been with the possessions retrieved from her ruined car, and it took him an instant too long to regain his focus on the conversation. She had always been excellent at distracting him.

"I've done more than enough of that over the past few weeks," he said.

Desdemona gave a half-smile, but it looked troubled. He began to move toward her slowly, giving her time to back away into her room if she chose. She didn't move. Instead, she held his gaze in silence, apparently waiting for him to speak.

Eddie cleared his throat and sought words that did their best to elude him. Since they'd entered separate cars at the warehouse, he'd wondered what he would say to her the next time he had the chance. In his mind, he had played out countless scenarios, and now he couldn't remember one of them.

"At the warehouse," he said finally, "I didn't get a chance to see if you were all right. We both had a lot to take in and process, and I know it was asking too much of you to pass judgment on me then. But I need you to know something and know that I mean it, from the bottom of my heart."

A frown slipped onto her features as he spoke. He knew she was probably trying to preempt him, to discern where the conversation was headed. Whether the wariness that crept into her expression was real or a product of his imagination, however, was unclear.

"Desdemona, I—"

"Desi."

The corner of Eddie's mouth twitched upward. She had never given him permission to call her by anything but her given name, apart from on the one night they had spent together. "Desi,"he repeated. He blinked, having temporarily lost his train of thought. "What I wanted to tell you..."

The way she stood—feigning ease but with her body radiating tension, clearly braced against whatever was to come—gave him pause. He knew, watching her, that she was not ready to hear what he truly wished to say. E-2 had scarred Desi deeply, and it would take much to undo what had been done. She was not ready to know that the feelings E-2 had felt for her were completely due to the place she held in Eddie's heart.

"...is that I'm sorry. I'm sorry for absolutely everything. For E-2, for Mia, for..."

She dropped her eyes, and he knew she was fully aware that her eldest brother's name would have been the next to enter the air. It was the fact that neither of them wanted to face—both the reason they were here together and the source of the almost tangible strain between them. He would do anything to take away the pain he had caused her. But though he would give his life for it, there was nothing within his power that could erase the damage.

"Listen to me," she said, looking up into his eyes with a new resolve. "I appreciate what you're trying to say. I really do. But you have nothing to be sorry for."

Eddie frowned. He opened his mouth to question her, but she continued.

"It wasn't you. You didn't kill… him. You didn't try to kill me. You didn't do any of the horrible things they did."

"But I created Mia," said Eddie gently, his eyes filled with sadness and regret. "And E-2. It's my fault—"

"No," said Desi shortly as she shook her head. "It's not your fault. Please, just let me believe that so I can sleep tonight."

Rendered speechless by the pain in her eyes, Eddie simply nodded.

"I think everyone needs their rest, if we're going to head out early."

Eddie hadn't seen Abigail move silently to stand in the shadows behind Desi. Only at her words did he notice her. She was indeed well-trained. He cleared his throat and straightened his posture, hoping Abigail hadn't heard too much of the conversation.

"Yes, you're right. Well, goodnight, Desi."

Without another word, he turned from them and retreated down the hall toward his room. He twisted the doorknob quietly and crept over the threshold, closing the door behind him.

"Late-night stroll?"

Lex's voice in the darkness startled Eddie, who jumped. He had thought the Division agent would still be asleep. It was then, with a dizzying pang, that Eddie realized Lex had probably never been asleep in the first place. He was there to keep an eye on Eddie, after all. Though it hadn't been explicitly stated by anyone, it was certainly true.

Eddie sighed. "You really don't trust me, do you? Any of you?"

Lex paused. "I'm trained not to trust anyone. It's nothing personal. And I do believe someone here trusts you, whether you see it or not."

Eddie crossed the room to his bed and lay down. "Who would that be?" he asked.

"I think you know. She seems to wish she didn't trust you, but she can't help it. She stole her brother's car and left the hospital on a hunch that that key might be something important from you. Think about it."

The thought brought a smile to Eddie's lips as he closed his eyes, hoping for sleep now that he had found a shred of peace.

Chapter Nineteen

The lobby was pitch-dark apart from the sparse light of streetlamps entering through the glass doors. Desi sat at the security desk, roving the room with panicked eyes. She knew something was terribly wrong. Slowly, she stood, and her gaze landed on a sight that she felt she had seen thousands of times.

Damian was slumped against the door, lifeless and still, two plasma wounds glaringly visible in his leg and chest. His sister fought the scream rising in her lungs as she turned away from him and toward where she knew she would find Lila holding the gun.

Lila was nowhere to be found.

Instead, Eddie stood where the android should have been, pointing the all-too-familiar weapon at the motionless Damian. Eddie's grey eyes were cold and severe, and there was a sickening darkness to them that sent a chill through Desi.

He lowered the weapon and turned to her. He met her gaze unflinchingly and moved with a purposeful stride to stand across the circular desk, where he paused.

"'Oh, that I were a glove upon that hand,'" he said, "'that I might touch that cheek.'"

Desi was frozen, unable to move even an inch as Eddie reached out a hand and placed it gently on the side of her face.

She shivered involuntarily, but she kept her eyes locked on his until he withdrew his hand, which she realized too late was covered with blood. Her own hand flew to her cheek, and she surveyed her fingers to find that they, too, were drenched in the horrid red liquid.

Eddie reached into his pocket and produced a small item that he concealed in his palm. He reached around Desi and fastened around her neck what she now realized was a thin silver chain. She looked down at what she knew to be the diamond solitaire necklace given to her by E-2, which gleamed preternaturally in the almost-nonexistent light. The clear stone's perfect appearance was marred by blood that spread onto Desi's chest where the solitaire lay.

Desi tore her eyes from the stone and focused again on Eddie, who grinned.

"Can you sleep, now?"

With a shriek, Desi awoke, one hand flying to her chest and the other to her cheek. Her breathing was ragged as she determined that the accursed necklace was nowhere to be found and that her hands were blood-free.

"What's going on?"

Abigail had appeared in a flash at her bedside, her expression panicked.

"It was…" Desi paused to take a deep, cleansing breath and let it out again. "It was just a dream."

"A pretty bad one, by the looks of it," said Abigail. "You're shaking."

A few moments passed in which Desi struggled to collect herself. She fought the trembling that had followed her into the waking world and pushed away the memory of the nightmare. *It wasn't real,* she told herself. *Everything is fine. Apart from the fact that Eddie has basically risen from the dead and we're being hunted by a group of crazy androids.*

"I'm all right," she assured Abigail in a tone she hoped was sufficiently convincing. "It was awful, but it's over."

The door burst open, and Derek stood on the threshold, visibly startled. "Desi? Are you okay? What is it—?"

"Derek, calm down." Desi pushed herself up onto her hands and met her brother's gaze. "I had a nightmare. I'm fine."

He hesitated, seemed to decide not to push the matter further, and then spoke again. "I came to tell you breakfast is ready. Leah sent me. Almost everyone is already downstairs."

Abigail nodded. "We'll be there shortly."

"We'll be waiting." Derek closed the door. The sound of his footsteps retreating told Desi that she and Abigail were alone again.

"What was the dream about?"

Desi sighed. She knew she could trust Abigail, but the thought of recalling the terrible scene she had witnessed in sleep was too much. "It's not important. Don't worry."

Abigail watched her carefully. "If you need to talk," she said after a moment, "just remember that I'll listen. Until then, let's go eat."

The Division agent led the way from the room and down the stairs. From there, the pair followed the sound of voices into a large dining room with a long oak table which, along with its matching chairs, hovered above the floor.

Most of their party was gathered around the table, while Ravenna, Leah, and Lila made repeated trips to the adjoined kitchen to bring out the abundance of food. The scents of morning filled the air. Coffee, bacon, eggs, pancakes, and toast were being served, and seats were saved for Desi and Abigail. One was between Charlie and Lex and the other between Derek and Eddie.

Desi knew which was for her. With a small sigh, she resigned herself to taking the allotted seat beside her brother and sat just as Ravenna laid a plate in front of her.

"Thank you."

Ravenna nodded. "Did you sleep all right?" she asked quietly enough for the others not to hear. "I heard people walking around at all hours. I guess it wasn't just me that had trouble getting used to being here."

Desi shrugged noncommittally. She opened her mouth to speak, but Kat addressed Ravenna from across the table.

"Do you mind if we turn on the news? I haven't heard a word from any of my contacts, and it's unnerving being so out of the loop."

"That's fine." Ravenna turned to retrieve the remote from the fireplace, and her mother handed the item to her as she passed. Ravenna slid it across the table to Kat, who turned on the telesense that hung on the wall behind Desi's side of the table.

The sounds of commercials mingled with the scraping of silverware and the passing of plates. Desi winced as Eddie's hand brushed hers. She then realized he was offering her the dish of pancakes, and she mumbled a small thanks while pulling two onto her plate. She ate silently, unwilling to engage in conversation. Derek still certainly doubted both the explanation for her scream and the reasoning behind her behavior the previous night, and the thought of an extended discussion with Eddie was no more appealing. The nightmare had shaken Desi deeply.

"This is Abdul Abaza for Channel Two News," said a somber male voice from the telesense. Desi listened intently, grateful for the distraction. "Before our commercial break, we received word that President Ethan McNaire, who we were last told was relatively stable after the assassination attempt of late last night, had gone into cardiac arrest."

Kat dropped her fork. The level of chatter buzzing through the room dropped considerably, and the group's collective focus began a steady shift to the screen.

"America, we have just been delivered heartbreaking news. As of 9:47 this morning, President McNaire is dead."

Desi whipped around in her chair at the same instant the dark-haired reporter disappeared behind a superimposed image of the late president, with "Ethan Arthur McNaire: December 18, 2168—August 11, 2232" emblazoned across the bottom.

In a flurry of motion, Kat leapt from her chair and produced her cell phone. She cried out in frustration. "No signal. No wonder Beck didn't tell me."

She stormed from the room, and Desi heard the front door open and slam. Lex followed Kat, while Casey stared icily forward and Charlie pushed her plate away and closed her eyes. Abigail placed an elbow on the table and rested her head in her hand. Leah stood frozen in the doorway with a plate of bacon. Aiden appeared behind her and glanced at the screen, and his expression turned grave. Ravenna lingered near the wall, her face blank.

"It's uncertain what caused the sudden change in the President's condition," Abdul continued, "but after he entered cardiac arrest, he became unresponsive to treatment, and it was only a matter of minutes before time of death was called. We have been told that McNaire's vice-president, Julius Hartford Cameron, was sworn in earlier this morning, following the shooting. Whether President Cameron will issue an official statement is unclear, but we have reporters en route to Washington, and we will issue updates as they become available."

"It was them, wasn't it?"

All eyes drifted to Lila, who had spoken to Charlie. The Division agent sighed.

"We don't know. Our people helped the FBI sweep the area after the shooting, but they found absolutely nothing. If I had to place money on it, though, I would say yes."

Desi's stomach lurched. West Point and the president within a day. If the androids had become this bold, she had no idea whether they still had limits at all. She returned her focus to the screen.

"In other news—" Abdul came to a screeching halt, and his eyes widened in what looked like terror as his hand flew to his earpiece. "Cut the camera," he instructed someone. "Switch to Skylar. Now."

A continual beeping wail sounded from the telesense, accompanied by a black display. No one moved. Then, suddenly, the emptiness was replaced by a dizzyingly unsteady view of a man the bar at the bottom of the screen identified as Skylar Ellis.

"We're coming to you live from Manhattan," said Skylar while he backed through a street packed with frenzied people. Smoke drifted on the air behind him, and when he came to a halt, it became apparent that the thick black cloud was emanating from a building Desi couldn't see properly through it. "We've just learned that Lawrence-Dodson Enterprises has been attacked."

An invisible weight crashed down on Desi, pressing her to her chair and removing all possibility of motion. Eddie was on his feet, and Derek dropped his plate to the table with a crash. In the corner of her vision, Desi saw Lila take Derek's hand.

The camera panned away from Skylar to focus on LDE. The glass doors of the first floor were blown out, as was all glass on the third, fifth, and eighth levels. Flames reached upward, climbing the building from the ignited floors. Through the smoke, people poured out from the wreckage of the ground level. They moved down through the stories like a scattered hive of insects fleeing for their lives.

"Four bombs have been detonated," said Skylar's voice over the pandemonium. "The NYPD has arrived, though they have given no clue as to who could be behind this attack. This news comes to us just hours after we reported that a hovercar belonging to Desdemona Lawrence had been recovered, having sustained critical damage. Miss Lawrence, newly-named Co-President of LDE, was nowhere to be found. Thus far, neither she nor her brother, Derek, one of the company's founders, has been seen in or coming out of the building. Employees we've spoken with have denied seeing either Lawrence sibling at work today, which leads us to believe that, while they may have been targets of the bombing, they were not injured in—"

Skylar was silenced by a series of immense blasts from behind him, and he whipped toward the explosions.

LDE was ablaze.

Desi watched in mute horror as the remaining floors were detonated one by one, the flames and smoke soaring to the sky as levels one through eighteen were ignited in a raging inferno.

Eddie lunged toward the screen. "No!" he cried, and the sound twisted something within Desi.

In a move that was more instinct than rational decision, she launched herself out of her chair and grabbed Eddie's arm. She held him back as the tears rolled freely down her cheeks. She had no idea when they had started, but she made no effort to fight them. At her touch, Eddie stopped trying to move toward the telesense. For what felt like endless moments, they were suspended there, unable to move. They simply watched as the building that encompassed several lifetimes' work was blown to oblivion.

"Turn it off," ordered Lila from behind them. Her tone was broken, but it carried an underlying harshness so unlike her that Charlie obliged without contention. The telesense went dark, and there was silence.

Desi watched Eddie closely. He stared after the image that had disappeared as though the intensity with which he did so could undo what he had seen. His heartbreak was visible in every line of his face, and Desi knew she could not begin to know this pain. While what she felt was excruciating, she knew only four who could know the depth of this loss, and one of them was dead.

Derek stood and moved wordlessly to his sister's side, Lila beside him.

"So this is what it feels like."

Desi looked once more to Eddie, who had spoken in barely a whisper.

"This is what it feels like to lose everything."

The front door opened, shattering the stillness following Eddie's words. Kat and Lex reentered the room and froze in their tracks upon seeing Desi, Eddie, Derek, and Lila standing in front of the telesense while everyone else remained ominously stagnant.

"What now?" Lex asked cautiously.

"LDE was bombed." Abigail spoke very quietly, but Desi knew it wouldn't have mattered. The words would have sounded like an explosion regardless of their volume.

A heavy sigh followed, along with the sound of someone sitting. Desi kept her eyes pointedly forward, her gaze boring an invisible hole in the wall behind the telesense. Sympathetic murmurs drifted on the air, and eventually, Kat spoke.

"I'm incredibly sorry for your loss," she told the small group as one. "But I'm afraid we don't have time to reflect on it here. We need to get to Washington as soon as physically possible. I've just been told that Blue Team has been designated President Cameron's private security detail for the time being. We're to protect him until the threat has been dealt with. So, if everyone will thank the Mitchells for their hospitality and get dressed, we need to go."

Hathor leaned against the railing with a practiced ease as her synthetic fingernails drummed a steady pulse against the metal.

She detested waiting. Why should she be made to wait for anyone, least of all a human?

"Which one of you was it?"

The voice came from behind and above her, from the top of the stairwell. Light filtered down the flight of steps from the door that led to the ground level and out of the decrepit tunnels Hathor's associates had taken to using to conceal their work. A moment of silence passed in which the human must have realized that Hathor had no intention of speaking with the door open, and a sigh echoed down the steps.

The door closed with a bang. Footsteps approached her in the darkness, and then he was at her side.

"Which one of you killed him?"

Hathor inhaled deeply at the voice of Harry Masters, former Division assassin and her current informant.

"Don't you think you're better off not knowing?"

A thoughtful pause followed. "Probably," Harry said at last.

She smirked. She knew he spoke of the human president Ethan McNaire. He didn't need to know which android had shot the man or which had finished the job in the hospital.

"How long until the next phase begins?"

"Patience," she said curtly. "Justice cannot be rushed."

"You might be interested to know that Hartley lied to you. Seward's team is not in Washington."

"What?" Hathor demanded. Her eyes narrowed, and her nails bit into her palm.

"Don't worry," said Harry patiently. "I've got it under control. I intercepted their transmissions, and I heard they've been assigned to guard the new president. They're on the way here, now."

Hathor let out a quick, relieved breath. Hartley and her lies would be dealt with, but at least the plan had only been delayed and not derailed. "Good," she said. "Osiris will be pleased to hear it. You continue to earn your place in our new order, my love."

Hands sought her out in the darkness and pulled her into an embrace.

"How long will we meet like this? How long will we live a lie?"

"The time for the truth is coming," she said, her tone reassuring. "I can't promise when it will be here, but it's coming."

"I trust you," said Harry. "That's good enough for me."

The instant he'd finished speaking, she felt the brush of his lips against hers. Barely an instant later, a loud crash from farther down the tunnel caused him to leap backward.

"Go," she muttered. "We'll meet soon."

Without another word, he started up the stairs. Light bathed the area once more and then disappeared along with the sound of his footsteps as the door closed.

"You know," Hathor mumbled into the darkness, "for someone who is in on the plan, it's obvious how much you don't want me to do my part in it."

"I know the role you have to play," said her mate as he appeared beside her, "but that doesn't mean I have to like it."

"Please, Horus." Hathor rolled her eyes. "You know you have nothing to fear. "You know you have nothing to be afraid of. You know I'm not interested in the human."

"But you play the part so well."

"Of course I do. It's the part I was created for. I was named for the goddess of love, remember?"

Horus grunted noncommittally. "Just remember what you're going to have to do, when the time comes. Our new order is no place for traitors."

Hathor's face fell, and she was glad the darkness obscured her. Yes, she knew what she would have to do. It had been part of the plan from the beginning. Then, she'd held no qualms with it. The human had betrayed the Division and his orders to kill Hathor, and he could never be fully trusted. But now, she wasn't sure she agreed with what she was supposed to do. Still, the double meaning of Horus's words was not lost on her.

If she turned her back on the plan their leader had devised, she would be the one without a place in the new order.

Chapter Twenty

Lila watched the buildings whip past as the car maneuvered through the streets of Washington, her expression carefully guarded.

Recent events had led her to question many things, not the least of which being herself. If E-2 had been the one to manipulate her instead of one of her creators, she had been reduced to a tool by two of her own kind, considering Mia's involvement. She had no idea how easy it would be for someone else to try something similar, but the thought that they could had set her on edge.

Since the first time she had been told of the seven androids commissioned by the Division, Lila had found them both intriguing and appalling. They have been design-ed to preserve human life—to defend the United States from attack and eliminate unnecessary risks to the lives of soldiers. Instead, these androids had killed. They had destroyed an entire town and slaughtered its inhabitants before being apprehended—captured, not killed, despite what Lila and the others had initially been led to believe. Apparently, the Division had retained a small amount of hope that the androids could be salvaged, repaired, and repurposed. Made suitable to live among humans, despite what they had done.

And now they were almost certainly responsible for the death of the President of the United States as well as the countless souls claimed at West Point.

Lila was a firm believer in second chances. After all, had Derek not allowed her that privilege, she might not be alive. If he had fallen for E-2's ploy, Derek could have killed Lila in retribution for the death of his brother. But whereas she had not been a deliberate danger to those around her, the Division androids most certainly were.

It was the same problem with Mia and with E-2, Lila thought. *They both lacked inhibition, like the Division androids. A sense of right and wrong. A boundary that they wouldn't cross. I, on the other hand, know what it is to be human—if not physically, at least in terms of morality. That is what separates me from them. A programming flaw.*

Though she knew this to be true, doubt had crept into the recesses of her mind. One minute flaw, one infinitesimal miscalculation, could lead her down a path from which there was no return. If something were to go wrong with her programming, what was to stop her from harming those she loved again? Her friends? Derek?

"Did you hear me?"

Lila blinked, drawn from her thoughts and back into the real world by his voice from the driver's seat.

"I didn't, I'm sorry."

"I said I think this is it. Kat stopped up there." He pointed out the windshield to where the Division agent had parked her car outside a nondescript building on the right-hand side of the street. Derek parked beside her, with Casey taking the space on Derek's right.

"Where do you think we're going?" Lila asked.

"I have no idea. Wherever it is, I'm sure it's better than the alternative."

A shadow crossed his handsome face, and Lila knew where his thoughts lay. They remained in New York, buried in what was surely now the rubble of what had once been LDE. She reached out and rested her palm against his cheek.

"We will find a way to fix this."

"Lila, it can't be fixed."

"Of course it can, Derek. I learned long time ago that you can do anything you so much as think about doing. You'll rebuild LDE and then—"

"What about rebuilding our lives?"

This gave her pause. She said nothing, electing to watch him until he continued. Derek was frowning, and his eyes were bloodshot.

"After all this, how can we go back to living the way we did before? Think about it for a minute. We know someone is after us. If we rebuild, what will stop them from coming again? From taking away our lives' work, again? After the things we've all done, how can we go back to pretending to be so naïve?"

"For whatever reason," said Lila, "the Division androids have it out for us. If we find a way to deal with them, we won't have anything to be afraid of."

"I think we should get out of the car."

Lila removed her attention from Derek and directed it to Ravenna, who sat in the back seat and had taken on a rather odd expression. It looked equal parts agitated and apprehensive.

"Kat's waiting for us, and we're under time constraints."

Derek nodded. "You're right. Let's go."

The three of them climbed out of the car. Lila looked to her left to find Kat, Lex, Abigail, Eddie, and Clarisse already standing on the sidewalk. Within moments, Desi arrived from the third car with Charlie and Casey.

Lex inhaled deeply. "Ah, the smell of corruption."

Desi smirked, and Abigail rolled her eyes.

"No," said the latter, "that's just you."

"Where are we going?" The question came from Ravenna and was directed at Kat.

"This way. Follow me, please."

Kat led them down the sidewalk until they reached an intersection, where the group crossed the street and continued for another block before Lila noticed exactly where they were. Up ahead, a large white obelisk rose into the afternoon air.

"The Washington Monument?" Lila asked aloud before she thought to stop herself.

Kat only shrugged. She led them to the monument's base, where she paused. After glancing over her shoulder and affirming that, apart from the intermittent tourist, they were alone, Kat produced a keycard. She ran it carefully down the corner of the stone tower. Lila watched, brow arched, as a miniscule green light flashed near where Kat had swiped the card. A click sounded, and Kat crouched, feeling along the ground until she found what she sought. She pulled upward on a tuft of grass to reveal a hidden door that led downward.

"In," she ordered. "Quickly."

One by one, the members of the group funneled into the hole and down the narrow metal steps it concealed, with Kat bringing up the rear. She closed the door, and the natural light dissipated, replaced by the artificial glow of lamps set into the walls of a long, otherwise-barren corridor.

Lila's body tensed. The memory of being trapped within West Point with no idea what was happening shot through her mind, and she ordered herself to relax.

"Could someone please explain why we're here?" asked Eddie, who looked thoroughly lost.

"There's a network of underground passages beneath the city," Kat explained. "Well, two. One is for the protection of the president and to make it easier for him to move from place to place in the event of an emergency, and the other is the subway system. We've just entered the first."

Eddie nodded, the set of his mouth indicating he was impressed.

"We're meeting some of the Division operatives stationed here, as well as the president. I would greatly appreciate it if everyone remains on their best behavior. Understood?"

Nods and mumbled assent spread through the group. Kat then turned to Lila.

"Forgive our operatives if they're a bit skittish around you when they realize what you are. It's nothing personal. We've just had our share of bad luck with androids."

"Okay." Despite her tranquil exterior, Lila was deeply disturbed by Kat's words. Was she to be treated as a hostile, simply because she had been created and not born?

Humans are so concerned with prejudice among themselves, she thought. *Can't they see when they inflict it on others?*

Kat squeezed her way to the front of the group and led them down the hall. As they walked, Derek slid an arm around Lila's waist. He leaned close and spoke quietly into her ear.

"I'm sure she didn't mean anything offensive by that," he said. "She just wants you to be warned in case some of their 'operatives' turn out to be idiots."

"How could it not sound offensive, Derek?" Lila whispered. "I can't help what I am, and I can't help what *they* are." She knew he would realize she was referring to those of her kind created by the Division.

"I know. Don't worry about it, all right? You don't need anything else to stress over."

And so he knows. He knows I've been hit hard by what's happened to LDE, too. Does he know how much I wish I was anywhere but here? Anywhere but running from some of my kind while trying to pick up the pieces they've left behind?

She couldn't ask him this. Not here, not now. Lila would share her fears another time, when they weren't surrounded by friends and potential enemies.

Kat opened the door at the end of the hall and motioned the group inside. Lila observed that they had entered a large room with thick concrete walls and numerous long, floating tables. It resembled a cafeteria without the food. When they had all entered, the door was shut, and Lila glanced from the members of her party to those who were already present in the room.

There were several people dressed in black attire similar to that of Blue Team; nondescript, not likely to draw unwanted attention in the outside world. A group of four lingered near the room's back corner. There were two men and two women, all of whom appeared roughly the same age. One of the men was leaning against a table with his arms folded. He had a sarcastic air about him, and he was speaking in a hushed tone with a woman with a high ponytail. The other woman sat in a chair with her nose buried in a book. The second man caught sight of the newcomers, locked gazes with Kat, and started toward her.

"You made it."

"You know me better than that, John. Of course we did. Everyone," she said, addressing Lila and the others, "this is John Beck. He's the contact I've been speaking with."

Beck smiled at them and gave a small wave. He was sharp-jawed with jet black hair and small eyes.

"It's nice to meet all of you. You seem to be acquainted with Blue Team." He indicated the rest of Kat's squad. "When I'm not serving as the Division's official political representative, I'm the head of another special operations group called Red Team. Guys."

The three people hovering in the corner snapped to attention and fell in at his side. As Beck introduced them, they each nodded in greeting.

"This is Angelina Beaufort." He placed a hand on the shoulder of the woman with the ponytail. "She may have been born French, but she's been quite an asset to the American military. And Nicolas Moretti..." He moved to the curly-haired man with the severe, square face. "His first experience with us was while he was deployed in China. One of our androids was causing trouble with his Army regiment. After that... 'situation' was taken care of, he joined us."

Beck stopped beside the final member of his team: a woman with a black choker around her neck. "Cleo Wolfe. She's the youngest, but she's wicked with a plasma gun."

Lila retained a small, polite smile as each of them was introduced. Her focus, though, was continually drawn to the man that was standing alone beside a table on the opposite side of the room. He was facing pointedly away from them with his arms folded across his chest. He wore a dark suit, and his brown hair was greying in streaks. He radiated a calm dignity that Lila couldn't quite place. Whoever he was, he possessed a tremendous amount of composure, and, she assumed, power.

Lila pulled her gaze away to meet Kat's, and her cheeks burned. Kat glanced at the man Lila had been watching, and understanding passed over her sharp features. She gave a small nod and cleared her throat.

"Special Agent Kathleen Seward of the Perfect Soldier Division's Blue Team at your service, Mr. President."

Mr. President? Lila's breath caught in her throat. She had known they were to meet him, but she hadn't expected it to happen like this. The man in question turned to acknowledge Kat with a respectful inclination of his head.

"It's lovely to meet you, Agent Seward. I appreciate your willingness to assist me in this… stressful time." He crossed the room to stand beside her, took her hand, and shook it. He then surveyed the remainder of the group. "Well, I recognize some of you. To those of you who don't know, I'm Julius Cameron. I know you're Derek Lawrence, you're Desdemona, and you're Lila." He greeted each of them in turn, and then his brown eyes fell on Eddie. Cameron frowned. "You're Eddie Dodson." He glanced to Kat for confirmation. "Am I missing something?"

Kat closed her eyes and nodded. "I'll brief you fully as soon as my team is settled in, sir. For now, suffice it to say that he isn't guilty."

Cameron raised an eyebrow and shrugged, offering a hand to Eddie. "That's good enough for me."

Eddie gave the president a small, anxious smile that suggested his high level of discomfort at the conversation and relief at the dropping of the topic. Cameron then turned to Ravenna.

"I don't believe I've seen you before, miss. You do remind me quite a lot of someone I know…" He searched the group, and his eyes alit on yet another member. "Ah, there's Clarisse. Are you two related?"

Ravenna nodded. "Yes, sir. She's my aunt."

"I see. You'll already have some knowledge of governmental affairs, then."

Ravenna stifled a short laugh. "That I do, sir."

He nodded thoughtfully. "Beck," said Cameron, addressing the leader of Red Team, "I would greatly appreciate it if you and your team could find accommodations for our guests."

"Certainly, sir. Blue Team and other Division personnel, follow me, please. Barring Kat, that is; I'll leave you to apprise the president of what's happening out there. You two gentlemen, please follow Nicolas, and Cleo and Angelina can escort the ladies." Beck saluted the president, turned on his heel, and led the Division members from the room.

"This way, please," said Angelina to Lila, Desi, and Ravenna. The group moved as one into the hallway, where the members diverged by gender. Kat was left alone in the room with the president.

"Before you go, can I speak with you for a moment?"

Lila turned to see Derek watching her carefully. His expression was reserved, and in his eyes, she detected the faintest hint of fear.

"Of course."

"I'll be right back," Derek assured a wary-looking Nicolas and a confused Eddie. Angelina folded her arms and appeared to be straining her patience to allow this delay.

Derek gave Lila a small smile and a nod, and then he took her arm and guided her around the corner and out of earshot of those who remained in the hall.

"I'm sorry I've been short with you," he said quietly. "I know this is every bit as hard on you as it is on me, and I really want you to know that I meant what I said no matter what else happens. I love you, Lila. And whether we have a company or not, that's still true."

Lila let out a long breath, the knot in her chest unwinding slightly.

"I feel the same way," she said. "And I just want you to know that whatever can be done to fix this, I'll do it. Anything."

"I know." He embraced her, and she held onto him tightly. She didn't know what awaited them with the Division, but for now, the fact that they had one another was enough.

In the dim light cast by the lamps set into the stone-grey walls, Clarisse sat in silence. She was alone at the table, and she did her best to disregard the pacing of the Division agents outside the room.

This mess is on my head, she thought solemnly.

"I'm fine," said a voice from outside. It was hauntingly familiar but hard to place, as though she had heard it only in a distant dream. "Thank you, but I don't need any help."

Clarisse looked up as the pieces clicked together in her mind. A figure moved through the doorway, caught in silhouette by the brighter glow outside. As it drew nearer, Clarisse found her suspicions undeniably confirmed. The figure was that of a woman in a hoverchair. Her hair was chin-length and red, and her blue eyes were aged far beyond her barely sixty years by an unmistakable pain and sadness.

"Hello, Isabella."

"Clarisse."

Isabella's chair propelled her forward into the room, where she stopped at the side of the table opposite where Clarisse sat. Their eyes met, and decades of secrets hung in the air between them, ominous and agonizing.

Clarisse gave her old friend a faint smile. "Welcome to the hell we created."

Isabella shook her head slowly. "We meant well. We could never have foreseen how badly things would turn out."

"No good deed goes unpunished."

Isabella sighed. "No, I suppose you're right. How many people have our creations killed, now? The Division is keeping me in the dark as much as they possibly can."

"You don't want me to answer that, Isabella. That I can promise you."

The time had long passed when Clarisse would have referred to Isabella Hartley as *"Madam President"* or *"ma'am."* Once, she had been the odher woman's advisor, and Isabella's word had been law. Upon Clarisse's promotion to President of the Division, the gap in their ranks had closed somewhat, but it was not until Clarisse had resigned from that post that she had dropped all formalities where her friend was concerned. They had seen too much—been through too much together—to require such proper displays. In truth, Clarisse's time with the Division had eroded much of her respect for Isabella and almost all she'd held for herself.

"I heard Susan Rush die, Clarisse. She was in my living room when they broke in and shot her. I hid, but why they didn't come for me, I'll never know. But I was shot in the spine at the end of my second term, and I would bet what's left of my life that they were behind it. I think I have a right to know who else they've destroyed."

Clarisse nodded stiffly, defeated. She could not bring herself to deny Isabella this. They had each lost so much that only the other had the ability to understand, and they owed one another any small form of assistance they could provide.

"Ethan's dead."

Pain flashed over Isabella's face. "I knew he was shot, but they didn't tell me he died."

Ethan McNaire had been Isabella's political rival and opponent in every major movement of her career even before her predecessor had named him Secretary of Defense. That same predecessor had waged the war that had led to the inception of the Division, which Ethan had vehemently opposed despite the fact that Isabella had allowed him to remain in her cabinet as a gesture of bipartisan good-faith. They had never been fond of one another, but Clarisse knew that Isabella had never truly disliked Ethan or wished him ill. She also knew the reverse could not be said, but she didn't want to further tarnish his memory in Isabella's eyes by repeating this. She continued her explanation.

"LDE headquarters has been wiped off the map. Mia was destroyed, but her body was taken. They blew up West Point, and they're hunting my niece. I have no idea what their endgame is, but I know this is just the beginning."

Isabella lowered her face into her hands, and her shoulders began to tremble. "We had no idea," she whispered. "We had no idea what we were going to cause."

"No, we didn't," said Clarisse. The ghost of a smile played on her lips. "I'm beginning to wish we'd asked them to build a time machine."

Chapter Twenty-One

"It's worse than we thought, Kathleen. Much worse."

With a heavy sigh, President Julius Cameron dropped the pretense of composure he had shown so perfectly to the others. He pulled a chair to the edge of the table nearest her and sat, motioning for her to do the same. Kat wasn't entirely certain why he was showing her this side of him. Had he reason to trust her more than any of the other Division personnel?

It could be due to her high standing within the organization; she was the leader of the most respected special operations team on the Division's payroll, and she had earned quite an outstanding reputation of her own in the service of her country. Then again, the president's suddenly relaxed demeanor around her could have more to do with her relationship to the Division's leader than with her own accomplishments. Rachel was well-liked by most government officials, though not at all so by Cameron's predecessor. The tension between Rachel and McNaire had been apparent to any poor soul who'd happened to enter a room occupied by both of them at once. Kat wondered what view Cameron held of her cousin.

Having once again found herself thinking of Rachel, Kat forced her thoughts back to the present time and location. She had lost countless hours of sleep worrying for her cousin's safety, not to mention the waking time she had spent in the same fashion.

"What do you mean, sir?"

"When we determined the androids were preparing to strike, we had no idea the scope of the attacks they were planning. Unfortunately, West Point was only the beginning."

Kat closed her eyes and lowered her head into her hands with a sigh of her own. She tensed her shoulders, bracing herself against the horror of the news her leader was preparing to impart. "What have they done now?"

"I trust you've heard what has become of the Lawrence-Dodson Enterprises installation in New York City." Upon Kat's grudging nod, Cameron continued. "That's not the only LDE facility they've attacked."

Kat's head snapped upward, and she stared at him. "How many?"

"All of them."

Kat blinked, uncomprehending. "Pardon, sir?"

"I believe you heard me correctly, Agent Seward. I said the androids have moved on every LDE location in the United States. Los Angeles, Albany, Miami, Orlando, Chicago, St. Louis… Ten locations in total, blown all to Hell."

Kat's throat was tight, constricted with emotion. This news would have been devastating on any given day, but with how well-acquainted she had recently become with the company's executives, the situation took on a new degree of tragedy in her mind.

"They don't know." It was a statement, not a question. She knew beyond certainty that Derek, Desi, Eddie, and Lila had no idea what had become of their company. If they had known, it would have shattered them by now.

"I would imagine not," conceded Cameron. "The New York attack was the first. I assume the androids knew that was where LDE started and wanted to make an impression. To incite fear. That, Agent Seward, is something I will not abide. Scare tactics and psychological warfare against the United States are things I will not bow to."

"I don't think they're expecting you to, sir. If it was a scare tactic, it worked. It was aimed at the Lawrences and Eddie Dodson."

At the mention of the final name, Cameron stiffened. "Speaking of Dodson, I believe you owe me an explanation, Kathleen."

She nodded solemnly. "It isn't one I fully understand, myself. Apparently, after the deaths of Senator Lawrence and his wife—caused by Mia, I might add—" Cameron flinched as the android's name entered the air, but Kat continued, "—Derek, Eddie, and Damian started experi-menting with the idea of preserving someone's memories in a non-human form. They started developing an android that was an exact copy of Eddie—"

"Cloning?" Cameron frowned.

"Basically," Kat admitted. "The only difference is that it isn't grown, it's built. But it had all of Eddie's memories and feelings and all that. It had a problem, though."

"If I had to put my money on what that problem was, I would have to guess it had something to do with a lack of inhibition that led the copy to do, ah, 'questionable' things."

"Yes, sir."

"Just like the Division's."

"Yes, except that E-2—the copy—didn't show any negative effects of this flaw until years after his creation. Admittedly, he was in cryogenic stasis for much of that time, but it wasn't until Mia incapacitated the real Eddie and switched him out with the copy that anything bad came of that programming issue. Mia managed to convince E-2 that killing Damian Lawrence was a good idea, and I'm sure you heard the rest of the story from the news and the tabloids. Mia and E-2 are both dead, now."

"I see. Does this mean the real Dodson isn't guilty of anything?"

A short laugh burst from Kat's lips. "If you consider aiding the Division wrong, then he's guilty as sin, just like we are. But as far as any actual illegal activities, no, he isn't."

"Then if in the course of your duties your run into any trouble with law enforcement regarding Dodson, consider this as his official pardon. I don't want any messes with classified information leaking in order to keep him out of prison, but a presidential pardon should be enough to shut up anyone who starts asking questions."

Kat nodded. "Of course, sir. I'll notify him."

She moved to stand, but he caught her arm. "Please do, but not yet. I have more to say before you go."

"Yes, sir." Kat retook her seat and folded her hands on the table, waiting for him to speak.

"As I've said, I will not be intimidated by these machines. I intend to prove to them and to the rest of the world that the United States of America is and will continue to be strong and that it has a cool head on its shoulders. I intend to hold a dinner and ball within the next several days, the proceeds of which will be donated to the rebuilding of LDE. In addition, Mr. and Ms. Lawrence, Mr. Dodson, the Misses Mitchell, and Lila will all be honored and welcomed guests."

Kat's jaw had dropped sometime around the phrase "dinner and ball," and she stared at the president with wide eyes. "You're not serious, sir?"

"As the grave, Agent Seward. And if the members of the Division choose to be present in full force, armed, with the knowledge of the situation at hand and the possibility of uninvited guests, then I would have no way to know of such things in advance and thus no reason to worry any officials within our government unnecessarily."

Shock washed over Kat, and she blurted out a reaction to the president's words before she could pause to consider whether he wanted one. *"A trap, sir?"*

A mischievous gleam entered his dark eyes, but his face gave no other reaction to her words. She might as well have made an offhand comment on the weather.

"I've said no such thing."

"Understood, sir." The corner of Kat's mouth twitched upward in a half-smirk.

"On the record, however, I would like to note that until your cousin resurfaces, you are promoted to acting head of the Division."

"Thank you." Kat's muscles tensed, but she forced away the reaction before she thought he would notice. She forced herself to relax and take a deep breath. *I can handle this,* she thought. *He said until Rachel resurfaces. This means he has at least some small amount of hope that she will.*

Cameron nodded. "I have the FBI and the CIA looking for her, and I don't plan to call them off anytime soon. I just want you to understand what we're up against here, Kat."

This first use of her preferred name tugged at Kat's heart. He was trying to connect with her, trying to warn her and protect her in some small way from the devastation that she would face if the search turned up nothing. She fought to swallow the lump rising in her throat and nodded stiffly.

"I do. But I want you to understand, sir, that I don't care what we're up against. I won't give up until no other option exists. As long as there is another way, another small chance that we'll find her, I won't stop believing that it will happen."

As Cameron nodded, Kat thought she saw a glint of pride enter his eyes.

"I would expect no less," he said.

"Thank you."

Kat pushed back her chair and stood. This time, Cameron did not move to stop her. He allowed her to make her way to the door and take her leave.

As long as there is the smallest chance, she thought as she wove through the tunnels to search out Blue Team, *I will keep believing that my cousin is alive.*

It was dark. At first, that was all Rachel knew. The feeling hadn't returned to her limbs—the oppressive numbness that she had come to call her reality held her immobile and threatened to pull her from consciousness once again.

Footsteps hurried toward her, and she wanted to turn away from them, to find some way to escape before they reached her. Her eyes ached, and she knew that if she could see her reflection, she would find mascara trails tracing her cheeks.

She hadn't given them the satisfaction of hearing her scream.

Light exploded around her now, and her hands moved on reflex toward her eyes, but brown leather wrist restraints held them firmly in place. The pain in her eyes multiplied a hundred fold as the light assaulted them, and she closed them in refusal to acknowledge whoever had entered the room.

"Well, she's alive," said the voice of Isis flatly.

"That's a step in the right direction." Rachel knew this voice belonged to Bastet, who sounded farther away from her than Isis had. "It's better than we hoped."

A hand closed firmly around Rachel's wrist. "Open your eyes. Now."

When she did not immediately oblige, Isis tightened her grip on Rachel's arm. Pain surged outward from the place the android gripped, and at last, Rachel surrendered. She opened her eyes to find the blond, sharp-chinned Isis standing over her where she lay on the table at the center of the concrete room. Bastet lingered a few paces behind, watching the encounter with hesitation. Rachel had no idea whether Bastet had been programmed with the ability to feel remorse or whether the android was simply wary of getting too close to the captive daughter of the president who had commissioned her.

Isis leaned forward, lowering her angular face to examine Rachel, who held Isis's gaze steadily, her hatred simmering just beneath the surface. She believed Isis saw it there. The android smirked and turned to her counterpart.

"Come look at her eyes."

Bastet gave a small nod and closed the distance between herself and the table. She stopped beside Isis and looked down at Rachel. Bastet's frighteningly bright emerald eyes widened, and she looked from Rachel to Isis and back again.

"Does this mean it worked?"

Before Isis could answer, a rough, pained cry sounded from outside. The androids exchanged glances and shot in a blur of motion out the door.

Rachel was left alone, the sound of her breathing her only company. After several seconds of unbearable quiet, shouts burst from another room.

"How could you let this happen?"

"Don't you dare blame me!"

"We took care of Hartley! This was your job!"

"There was nothing she could have done!"

Another sharp cry followed, longer than the first and full of agony. The shouted argument subsided immediately, the voices Rachel recognized as belonging to Isis, Hathor, Bastet, and Horus giving way to the pain of another, which was also familiar. Rachel's weary mind processed at last what it had failed to grasp after the voice's first cry.

"Andrew!" Rachel struggled violently against her restraints. *"Andrew!"* The tight leather straps began to give, and her resolve doubled as the idea of freedom became slightly less impossible.

"No, leave her. She isn't a threat. Not yet, anyway."

"If she realizes what she can do, she will b—"

"Hathor, shut him up. She can hear, now, remember?"

"We're losing him," said Bastet in a small voice.

Rachel wept, her breathing shallow from her struggle. Biting her cheek to suffocate the strained yell that wanted to burst from her lungs, she wrenched her arms upward, pulling the restraints free of the table. She stared at the leather cuffs encircling her wrists and the snapped metal links that had held them in place.

In the other room, the androids had fallen silent.

They already know I'm trying to get free. And they have Andrew. What more can they take from me?

With this thought at the front of her mind, Rachel sat up quickly and bent forward to find her ankles similarly restrained. She grasped the straps and pulled at them with all her strength, and they gave much more easily than the first pair had. The force she exerted on them was greater than necessary, and they flew from her hands and over her shoulders, thumping to the floor behind the table.

Trembling, Rachel stood.

Why was that so easy? I shouldn't have been able to do that.

"Wait a second, come back here, he's—damn it, Horus, we lost him."

Rachel's heart sank, leaden, to the pit of her stomach. Her fear evaporated instantly, and she burst from the room toward the voices.

The air was heavy with an old, dry smell Rachel couldn't place. Her eyes adjusted rapidly to the darkness of the tunnel, much to her confusion, and she processed the sight of a track laid into the ground that seemed to move in an endless straight line. She followed the track and a light several yards down to her left, and they led her to a cracked door. She gave it a small push, and it swung open.

Andrew lay unmoving on a perfect double of the table Rachel had just occupied. Hathor was bent over him, one of her hands entwined with Horus's. The latter was a few steps closer to the door than the former, as though he had been on his way out. Bastet stood on Andrew's other side, her hand closed around his wrist as though she had been checking his pulse. Isis stood at the foot of the table, watching the others with half-concealed sadness.

Why do they look like they care about him?

Before another thought could pass through Rachel's mind, Horus whipped toward her.

"Not to be rude, love," he said to Hathor, "but I told you so."

Hathor stiffened and stretched to her full height, turning to face Rachel with a question in her cold emerald eyes. Her red lips were pressed together in firm calculation. She took a step forward, which Rachel mirrored with a step backward.

"There's no point in trying to run," said Horus flatly. His sharp nose and narrowed eyes gave him the look of a predatory bird preparing to strike. "You won't get far."

"Then why do you all seem so afraid of what I know?" Rachel's eyes flicked from Horus to Andrew, and she was unable to hold herself back any longer. She launched forward, pushing past Horus and Hathor and ignoring the red flags raised in her mind by how easily they were moved by her shoves.

She flung herself down at Andrew's side, kneeling and leaning over him to examine his pale face. She laid her shaking hand on his cold cheek. A terrible sob ripped its way from her lungs, and she dropped her head onto his chest and closed her eyes.

"How could you do this to him?"

"We tried to save—"

"Hathor." Isis cut her off firmly.

"To answer your question, Ms. Hartley," said a voice from behind Rachel, "killing is what we were built to do."

She did not look up; she knew that if she turned, she would find Osiris. The sound of footsteps followed his words, and he entered Rachel's line of sight when he stopped beside Isis. He met Rachel's eyes, and he faltered for only the slightest fraction of an instant. Then he spoke again with a cool calm that was unnerving as she sat weeping over Andrew's body.

"We followed orders," said Osiris, "when we were born. I suppose you could say our flaw was that we followed them too well. It was doing what the Division told us that led to our downfall. We received an order to end a threat, and we succeeded. We also managed to ensure that the threat would have no way to begin again. But that wasn't good enough for them. No, they saw only that we had killed. That we had taken the lives of more humans than they intended. Do you know who gave us the order to kill, Rachel?"

She did not answer. She held his gaze evenly through her tears, trying not to stare at the jagged scar tracing from his left temple to the corner of his mouth.

It seemed the Division's creations had all fallen into the same trap. She recalled the day she'd taken over the organization, when she'd learned about Mia, who had been responsible for countless deaths even before she'd participated in the highly publicized murder of Damian Lawrence.

Like Ra, one of the original seven androids commissioned by Rachel's mother, Mia had since been killed. Unfortunately, six remained.

"I know you do," Osiris pressed. "It was your mother, Isabella. And Clarisse. They told us to kill, and we did. They created us, you see. We were everything they wanted and more. But then they didn't want us. We were too good at what we were created to do. And do you know what else the Division did? Of course you do. It wasn't under your watch—Clarisse was still running the farce of an organization when they attacked—but you've picked up the pieces nicely over the last several years. They had the nerve to try to slaughter us. And we will not allow Ra's death to go unpunished."

He looked up, then, away from her. His hate-filled green eyes roved from one android to the next, and Rachel noticed then that Anubis had entered the room.

"You've taken your revenge!" she shouted. "You've picked off the assassins one by one, and you've burned West Point to the ground! What more do you want?"

Osiris smiled darkly and shook his head. "Yes, we have. Most of the assassins are dead. However, Ravenna Mitchell lives, and she is the one responsible for Ra. The others were unimportant collateral damage."

Rachel leapt to her feet and rushed toward Osiris. In a flash, Horus and Hathor grabbed her arms and pulled her backward.

"Andrew is not 'unimportant collateral damage,'" she spat venomously. "I loved him!"

Osiris smirked at her from the end of the table. Beside him, Isis watched Rachel with a measured reproach.

"There's the fire we're looking for," said Osiris, nodding his approval.

With an enraged cry, Rachel wrenched her left arm forward, dragging Hathor with it. The android flew through the air and landed with a thud atop a startled, livid Horus. Rachel took a step toward the pair at Andrew's feet.

"Stop her." Osiris's tone was uninterested, but his eyes were intrigued.

Suddenly, pain splintered through the back of Rachel's head where Anubis had stricken her, and the room swam before her eyes. She slipped to her knees and then fell forward, catching herself against the cold concrete with her palms and unsteady arms.

The blurry outline of Osiris moved toward her. When he spoke, it was as though he were addressing her from the other end of a long, dark tunnel.

"You'll be too good at your job, too. I'm counting on it."

Her arms quaked and gave in to the strain, and she fell to the floor.

"You're going to save us."

The room spun a final time, and the blurred figures of the six androids and the man Rachel loved faded into darkness.

About the Author

Mandi Jourdan studied English and Classics at Southern Illinois University, through which she wrote and performed in two adaptations of the Harry Potter books in the style of Shakespeare. When not writing science-fiction and fantasy and listening to eighties rock, she spends time with her cats.

She can be found on Amazon, at
bloodandtalons.wordpress.com
or on Twitter **@MandiJourdan**.

WINTER 2017
APHOTIC REALM PRESENTS...
SHADOWS OF THE MIND
A Collection of Short Stories
MANDI JOURDAN
WWW.APHOTICREALM.COM

LACRIMOSA

a novel

Mandi Jourdan